Heaven Scent

Heaven Scent

REBECCA
CORNISH TALLEY

Bonneville Books
Springville, Utah

The views expressed within this work are the sole responsibility of the author and do not necessarily reflect the position of Cedar Fort, Inc., or any other entity.

This is a work of fiction. The characters, names, incidents, places, and dialogue are products of the author's imagination, and are not to be construed as real.

ISBN 13: 978-1-59955-100-5

Published by Bonneville Books, an imprint of Cedar Fort, Inc., 2373 W. 700 S., Springville, UT, 84663
Distributed by Cedar Fort, Inc., www.cedarfort.com

LIBRARY OF CONGRESS CATALOGING-IN-PUBLICATION DATA

Talley, Rebecca Cornish.
  Heaven scent / Rebecca Cornish Talley.
    p. cm.
  Summary: As her father's career-obsessed life threatens to break up their family, high school senior Liza finds comfort in playing basketball and discovering the Book of Mormon until tragedy strikes.
  ISBN 978-1-59955-100-5
  [1. Family problems—Fiction. 2. Basketball—Fiction. 3. Mormons—Fiction. 4. Coming of age—Fiction.] I. Title.
  PZ7.T1567He 2008
  [Fic]—dc22
                                        2007045312

Cover design by Nicole Williams
Cover design © 2008 by Lyle Mortimer
Edited and typeset by Annaliese B. Cox

Printed in the United States of America

10 9 8 7 6 5 4 3 2 1

Printed on acid-free paper

Dedication

FOR MY CHILDREN, Clayton, Angela, Rachel, Olivia, Logan, Madolyn, Savannah, Noah, Emma, and Jared, who are my treasure and my joy, and whose creativity has always inspired me.

FOR MY HONEY, DEL, who has always encouraged me to spread my wings and soar toward my dreams.

FOR JEANNIE, now on the other side, who first saw my flicker and ignited the flame.

FOR MY MOTHER, whose fragrant visits have strengthened me and my testimony and inspired this story.

FOR ALL OF THOSE WHO HAVE HELPED ME ALONG THE WAY.

Chapter One

Liza tucked the basketball under her left arm and then formed a *T* with her hands.

"Time out, Aldrich Heights," the tall, thin referee shouted as he pointed to Liza's team.

Liza and her teammates ran off the court to meet their coach by the bench. Liza caught a glimpse of her mom and brother in the bleachers. Where was her dad? She'd begged him to come to her game and he'd said he would. Why wasn't he there?

Coach Anderson tapped her on the shoulder. "Liza, pay attention. This is it. We have possession. We need to run the clock down. Leave only enough time to take one last shot. We can win this game."

The girls nodded.

Liza glanced at the doorway and then back to the bleachers, but she couldn't see her dad. Her stomach tightened.

Coach Anderson turned to Tamika. "I want you to throw the ball in to Liza."

"Okay," Tamika said.

Liza clenched her jaw. How could her dad miss this game?

"Liza, you take the last shot."

"Huh?"

"Focus, Liza. We're all depending on you. Can you handle it?"

Liza blinked her eyes. "Yeah."

"Are you sure?" Coach Anderson asked.

Liza turned to her coach. "Yes." She wiped the sweat from her face.

The buzzer sounded the end of time out. Liza's team returned to the court.

"With ten seconds left on the clock, Aldrich Heights High has the chance to score and win this championship game," the announcer boomed.

The referee handed the ball to Tamika and the sound of his whistle bounced off the walls of the immense gymnasium. Tamika threw a sharp pass to Liza. Liza glanced at the court clock. Ten. Nine. Eight. It was now or never. Driving toward the basket was her only choice. Her team trailed Roosevelt High by only one point and she couldn't afford to waver, not even for a second. It was up to her. She had to win this game.

She dribbled past center court.

"Time is ticking," came the announcer's voice.

Seven. Six. Liza narrowed her eyes. Several girls stood between her and the basket, but no one would stand in the way of her goal. Five. Four. She inhaled deeply, darted toward the key, and took her best jump shot.

Whack. She felt a stinging sensation as rough hands slapped her hand and arm. The shrill sound of the referee's whistle ripped through the air as she watched the ball bounce out of bounds.

"Foul on number two-one. Number fourteen, you're at the free throw line," the ref shouted above the jeering crowd. He handed the ball to Liza.

The announcer's voice cracked as he said, "Liza Compton's been fouled. Time has run out. This free throw will determine whether or not Aldrich High is still in the race for the California State Girls' Basketball Championship."

His words echoed in her ears. The beads of sweat pooled and trickled down her forehead. She licked her lips. This was the moment. Missing was not an option. She blew through her mouth, ran her fingers through her wet bangs, and cleared her mind.

The crowd for the opposing team whistled and hollered. Someone screamed, "You'll never make this shot."

Somebody else yelled, "You'll miss!"

Her heart pounded. Carefully, methodically, she took aim. She locked her sight on the goal. She bent her knees, jumped up, and followed through with a flawless arc of her right hand.

A hushed silence fell over the crowd as the ball neared the basket, hit the rim, and bounced straight up. Liza bit her lower lip, her gaze fixed. In slow motion, the ball descended and finally swooshed through the net. She exhaled and let her head fall forward. The home crowd exploded in applause and cheers. The score was tied.

The announcer cleared his throat and said, "If she makes this next basket, Aldrich Heights High School will have its first ever championship in girls' basketball."

The fans cheered. The referee again handed the ball to Liza.

She bounced the ball three times and listened to its echo as it mimicked her own heartbeat. Basketball was the one thing in her life that she controlled, the one thing she understood, her constant. While everything and everyone else changed, basketball remained the same.

Liza's head felt as if it were going to explode. This one free throw meant the difference between euphoric victory and endless regret.

In a low voice the announcer said, "This is the most important shot of Liza Compton's basketball career."

Liza held the smooth, round ball in her hands. For a brief moment, her concentration slipped while she searched the stands, hoping her dad would finally be there. Row after row she scoured the spectators. She glanced over at the double doors. Her gaze met her mother's. Her mom gave a faint smile and shook her head. Liza knew exactly what that meant. How could he? Again.

She gritted her teeth and forced herself to focus only on the task ahead of her. She stared at the goal. This was the basket everyone would remember. She'd scored twenty-nine points for her team, a personal best, but none of that mattered. It didn't even matter that she'd just made the free throw to tie the score. She had to make this basket. Her future depended on it.

She took her stance and let the ball go. It arched perfectly in the air. She watched and exerted all of her mental effort in willing the ball to the basket. She cracked her knuckles.

Once again, the ball hit the rim. It circled and circled and then circled some more. Around and around and around. She reached down to wipe her moist hands on her shiny red shorts. After what seemed like an eternity, the ball fell into the basket.

The home crowd burst into celebration. Old and young alike jumped to their feet and cheered. The audience was awash in varying shades of red and blue. Liza leapt into the air and screamed. Relief, joy, and excitement washed over her while her teammates rushed her like a mindless mob, practically knocking her to the ground.

"You are part of history tonight. Aldrich Heights has won the state championship!" the announcer yelled over the noise of the crowd.

"Way to go, Liza!" Megan screamed, her long red braids bouncing from side to side.

"We did it!" Liza exclaimed. She picked up Megan and spun her around.

"We're number one!" Tamika sang out in her high-pitched voice.

Sara danced around Liza with her finger held high in the air.

Liza raised her arms and waved them wildly.

The trombones, horns, drums, flutes, even the tuba, broke into the school song. Cymbals punctuated the chorus. Many students joined hands or linked arms and swayed back and forth to the beat of the band.

Cheerleaders, in their short white skirts and bright red and blue tops, jumped into the air and clapped their hands under one leg and then the other. The mascot, a white tiger dressed in a red vest with tails, ran across the expansive gym floor doing back flips, front flips, and cartwheels. Others in the crowd chanted.

Liza soaked it all in. She wanted to savor every glorious moment and lock each second into her memory.

She watched the disappointment on the faces of her opposing team. She felt sorry for them because she knew how important it was to win this game. Despite her empathy, she grinned so wide it hurt her face.

The losing team, in their green and yellow uniforms, banded together and gave a forced yell of congratulations.

A floating red-and-blue Frisbee caught Liza's gaze. She looked upward toward the soft glow of the fluorescent lighting and then at the towering mass of grandstands spread across the light, highly polished wood floor. She stared at the black scoreboard with the flashing red lights signaling the final score of fifty-seven to fifty-six. She closed her eyes and drew a deep breath through her nose to memorize even the smell of the multitude that shared her victory.

While she absorbed every drop of the unfamiliar gymnasium, she hoped she would make this gym her home court and play basketball for Oak University next year. Oak's strict entrance requirements and prestigious girls' basketball program seemed out of reach to Liza, but, for a moment frozen in time, she could immerse herself in all the sights, smells, and sounds of this gym, this night.

"Liza, what're you doing?" Sara asked. She grabbed Liza's long dark ponytail and pulled her down a few inches.

"Oh, sorry, Sara, I was . . . taking it all in, I guess," Liza said, rising to her full five-foot, ten-inch height.

"Can you believe this?" Sara exclaimed. She smiled and exposed her braces.

"Not really." Liza shook her head.

"This has never happened before. We'll be famous!" Sara giggled, jumping up and down.

Liza joined her.

Coach Anderson's sparsely covered head towered above the throng as he made his way through to Liza. He embraced her. "Definitely your best game. You didn't crack under pressure. Great job." He flashed his friendly smile.

"Thanks."

"Can we have all of the team members join us over here for the presentation of the trophy?" a female voice announced over the sound system. Liza recognized the stout woman as the district superintendent.

The team stood in a semicircle around a man in his mid-fifties who held the award. Sara elbowed Liza and said, "Is this awesome or what? Did you get a look at that enormous trophy?"

"I'm still in shock," Liza said while trying to smile for the cameras.

Sara whispered, "I knew you could do it. Ever since I met you at the beginning of the year, I knew you'd be the star of the team. We could never have won this championship without you."

"I don't know about that."

The older man spoke into the microphone, "Coach Anderson, it's my privilege to award you this trophy in recognition of winning the California State Girls' Basketball Championship. Your team played well. Congratulations."

The crowd went wild. Liza's smile widened. She'd never known such a sense of accomplishment, and she wanted to bask in it as long as possible.

Coach Anderson stepped over to the gentleman and took the trophy in his hands. He stared it at for a moment and then raised it above his head. The crowd erupted again.

After a few moments, Coach Anderson held his hands up to quiet the group. "Thank you so much for your support throughout this season. And thank you to my championship team. I'm so proud of each of you. You worked together better tonight than I've ever seen you. You all deserve congratulations. Let's meet over at Pizza Palace and celebrate in style." He held the trophy with one hand, high above his head, and pumped it several times.

The girls shouted their agreement. Camera flashes illuminated the gym while the school band played in the background. A loud hum of congratulations hung over the crowd.

Liza's mom and Jason finally broke through the swarm that surrounded Liza. "Oh, honey, you were so, oh . . ." A tear streamed down her mother's cheek. She reached for Liza's hand.

"Thanks, Mom." Her own eyes filled with tears.

"You were pretty awesome tonight," Jason said. He smiled and slugged her in the arm.

Liza punched him back.

Her mom stepped closer. "You did so well. I worried about that last free throw, but I knew, deep down, you'd pull it off. I'm so proud of you." She hugged her and whispered "I love you" in her ear.

Though she was ecstatic about winning, the stark reality of her father's absence hit her hard. Liza pulled away. "Where's Dad? He promised to be here."

Her mother smiled and pushed a lock of her own auburn hair behind her left ear. She removed her glasses and said, "I know he meant to—"

Liza cut in, "C'mon, Mom. He promised. The absolute most important game of my life. He promised he wouldn't let work get in the way. I told him so many times how much I wanted him to be here tonight."

"Liza, please, don't get upset. Not now. Be happy about your game. We'll discuss this later."

Liza's throat tightened. She wanted to scream at her mother, who maintained a pleasant, if not emotionless, expression—a talent her mother had seemed to perfect since moving to Aldrich Heights.

Liza covered her face with her hands and tried to control the rage and utter frustration that churned inside of her.

Liza's mom, who stood slightly shorter than Liza but quite a bit heavier, grabbed Liza by the shoulders and said, "Liza? Look at me. I want to see your beautiful blue eyes."

Liza continued to bury her face in her hands.

Her mother became more insistent and the tone of her voice changed. "Liza, I mean it. We'll talk about this later."

Liza removed her hands from her face. She watched her mother's practiced smile and even noticed a few wrinkles around her mother's eyes.

Jason broke in, "Don't let him wreck your night."

Liza inhaled deeply and blew the air out slowly through her mouth. She smoothed her hair and used her fingers to comb through her bangs. She wiped at her cheeks and licked her lips. She turned back to her teammates and, with a smile, said, "Pizza Palace, here come the champs." She darted toward the lockers with her team falling in line behind her.

Inside the large locker room, Liza sat on the cold wooden bench and stared at the ground. She wanted to be left alone to stew in her anger.

"What are you doing? We need to get over to Pizza Palace," Sara said.

Liza shook her head. "Huh?"

"Come on. Get with it." Sara pushed Liza's shoulder.

Liza wanted to smack Sara for bugging her. Sara always intruded in her space and asked annoying questions that were none of her business. She wished Sara would disappear so she could sort out her thoughts. "Give me a minute."

"If you don't hurry, I'm going to get everyone to come back in here and get you," Sara said as she ran off.

Liza rolled her eyes. She recounted her dad's promise to attend her game. Why did she believe him? Why did she continue to think he meant what he said? He'd let her down time and time again over the last year or so. But this was too important. This was her championship game.

Liza stood and hit the locker with the palms of her hands. She'd practiced all these years for this very moment, and he missed it. If he'd just for one minute put their family ahead of his career, he'd feel differently. He'd act differently. Their family would be important to him again. She'd be important to him again. But it didn't matter because he'd made the same choice. Again.

Now it was time to do something, instead of overlooking it as her mother always seemed to do. She needed to take action and make him realize what he was doing to their family.

Everyone expected her at Pizza Palace, and she deserved to celebrate, but she wanted to yell at her dad for, once again, sacrificing her for his job.

She pulled out her cell phone and was just punching in his number when Sara rushed inside with several of their teammates close behind her.

"We've come to get you, like I said." Sara pulled at Liza's arm.

Chapter Two

"I've already left three messages on your cell, Dad, and I keep getting the after-hours message on your office phone. Where are you? You've missed the game. Now we're going to Pizza Palace. Can you at least make it to the restaurant?" Liza slammed her phone closed and threw it on the front seat of her car.

She exited her car and ran across the parking lot to the front doors of the restaurant. She opened the doors and squeezed through the sandwich of people that overflowed the restaurant. She found Sara.

"What took you so long?" Sara questioned.

Liza shrugged. "Nothing. Absolutely nothing."

"Can you hear me?" Coach Anderson struggled to gain the crowd's attention in the restaurant. He played with the top button of his shirt.

Someone whistled and then yelled, "Quiet, everybody."

Coach Anderson raised his hands in the air. "If you'll allow me, I'd like to say a few more things, please." He turned to his team and said in his tenor voice, "You girls were fantastic tonight. In all my years of coaching, I have never had this experience before. Thank you." He turned to the group. "Thanks for your support and help through the season. I really mean this from my heart. And thank you, Liza, for not cracking."

Liza smiled.

The audience applauded and someone shouted, "Speech, speech, speech." Liza hesitated but, with insistence from her coach, stood on a chair.

Her face warmed. "Thanks. But it wasn't only me. We all won tonight." The crowd clapped. Liza continued, "If ever I shoot two free throws that hit the rim again, I'm through." The audience laughed and Liza stepped down.

Coach Anderson raised the trophy and said, "Isn't this the most beautiful thing you've ever seen?"

The crowd cheered.

"I know right where we'll put it too. We've won the state championship." He grinned.

Everyone broke into thunderous applause. They let out hoots and hollers of agreement.

Coach Anderson raised his hand and said, "Again, thanks for all of your support. The team and I really appreciate it. Please, enjoy yourselves and eat, eat, eat."

Liza grabbed four slices of pepperoni pizza and headed to a booth where Sara and Tamika sat.

Tamika scooted over and Liza sat next to her. She took a bite of her pizza and searched the room. Somehow, maybe, her dad would show up. She'd left enough messages on his voice mail.

She knew, in her head, that she was only setting herself up for disappointment, but she still hoped, in her heart, that he'd listen to his messages and make an appearance. After all, this was the most important night of her life, and he wouldn't miss all of it, would he?

"What's your answer?" Tamika asked twirling her kinky black hair around her finger.

"My answer for what?" Liza straightened the collar of her white polo shirt.

"Hello? We asked if you wanted to have a party at Sara's. We could party all night long," Tamika said, her dark brown eyes dancing from side to side.

"My mom said it was okay with her as long as we keep the music down and don't trash the house too much. What about it?" Sara leaned forward and tossed her bleached blonde hair behind her shoulders.

"I don't know." Liza continued to scrutinize the packed restaurant.

"You don't know? What kind of answer is that after what we've done tonight? We should be partying all night long, all day long, in fact, all week long," Tamika said. She pounded the table with her spoon and fork.

"Yeah, sure. I'll ask my mom." Liza grabbed her straw.

"Don't get too excited. I mean, we can only take so much enthusiasm," Tamika complained, scowling.

Liza shot her a look.

"I saw your mom and your brother, but I didn't see your—" Sara started to say.

Liza cut her off. "Yeah, so?" She twisted her straw and threw it across the table.

"Whoa, calm down," Tamika said. She blinked her eyes several times.

"Sor-ry. Hey, check out all the people that are here," Sara said.

Liza picked up her glass of soda and surveyed the room again. Although she'd only attended Aldrich Heights High since the fall, she recognized many of the students. Her gaze settled on a familiar face.

"I knew you'd find him," Sara said in a wispy voice.

"What're you talking about?" Liza asked sharply.

"Kyle Reynolds, of course."

"You've been crushing on him forever," Tamika said.

"No, I haven't." Liza played with her fork.

"Yeah right." Sara flipped her hair with her left hand. "We believe that."

"You watch him every time he walks by us," Tamika said,

"and you look like this." Tamika made her eyes big, stared at the table, and let her mouth drop open.

"Do not."

"C'mon, Liza, admit it. You think he's hot," Sara said. She pulled her glass close, put her straw in her mouth, and slurped the rest of her soda.

"You're so loud and obnoxious," Liza said.

"Don't look now, but I think Kyle's on his way over here with Jessica Landers and Natalie Hanks," Tamika said.

Liza looked at the table. What would she say if he actually spoke to her?

"Great game. You were pretty amazing," Kyle said.

Liza glanced up. Her words caught in her throat and her hands began to shake. Finally, she managed to eke out, "Thanks."

"You were all great," Jessica said.

"Yeah, I can't make a basket ever. I felt so stressed for you, Liza, but you were awesome," Natalie said.

Kyle smiled and Liza's heart squeezed tight. She watched him as he turned and walked away from the table.

"Here's a napkin to wipe up that drool," Sara said. She and Tamika laughed and pushed each other.

"You're so funny," Liza said.

"And you don't have a crush on Kyle, right?" Tamika pried.

"Right." Liza said it louder than she expected.

Her face felt hot. She'd noticed Kyle at one of the swim meets right after school started. He was perfect. His shiny blond hair and sky blue eyes made her pulse race. She only admired him from afar, though, because everyone knew that he was religious and only dated girls that attended the Mormon Church, like Jessica and Natalie. Someone even told her he planned to go on some sort of a mission or something for his church after everyone graduated in a few months. Though she wasn't Mormon, and didn't know much about Mormons, he still captivated her.

"Your face is bright red," Sara said.

Liza covered her cheeks with her hands.

"Where were you?" Tamika asked with a grin.

"Nowhere."

"Uh huh," Sara said.

"There's your mom and your brother over there," Tamika said pointing her chin in the direction of the door.

"Your brother is so hot. I love his long bangs. He's beautiful," Sara said wistfully. She smacked her lips as Liza's mom and Jason approached the table.

"Hello, Mrs. Compton." Sara said sweetly. "Hi, Jason." She eyed Jason up and down.

"Hello, girls," Liza's mother replied.

"Mom, Sara's having a party at her house tonight to celebrate. Can I go and spend the night?"

"That'd be fine. What time will you be home in the morning?"

Liza looked at Sara, who shrugged her shoulders. "I don't know, ten o'clock maybe," Liza said. She stood. "I'll be back in a minute. I need to talk to my mom." She walked toward the restaurant's front doors. Her mother followed behind her.

Liza spun around. "Where's Dad? He won't answer his phone."

"I don't know."

"He promised he wouldn't do this again."

"I know, but he's so busy right now."

If Liza had heard this excuse once, she'd heard it a thousand times. "He's always busy. I've left him a bunch of messages to come over here." Liza scrutinized the room. "But I don't see him. Do you?"

Her mother stepped closer to her. "Don't take that tone with me."

Liza's face burned. Her mother always defended her dad, and she was sick and tired of it. "Well—"

"I'm going to take Jason and go home. I'll see you in the morning."

"But—"

"I will not discuss this here. Go back to your friends and have fun at the party."

"Right. Whatever you say, Mom." She clenched her fists and marched back to the table. As she passed Jason, they exchanged glances and she shook her head.

She sat at the table and watched them leave. Anger boiled inside and threatened to surface, but she took a deep breath and convinced herself to settle down.

Sara fanned herself with her hand. "Whew! Your brother is so hot, even if he's only a sophomore. I could get lost in those light blue eyes. And his body is so fine. Must be from all that beach volleyball," Sara said.

"Jason? Hot?" Liza rolled her eyes.

"And his hair . . . I love how he flips his bangs back. Hot, hot, hot," Sara said.

"You think every guy is hot," Tamika said.

While Sara and Tamika argued over Tamika's claim, Liza thought about how, once again, her dad had performed his disappearing act. The more she thought about it, the more she wanted to scream at him. She reached for her cell phone, but realized she'd left it in her car.

"Sara, I need to use your phone."

Sara tossed her phone to Liza.

Liza punched in the numbers and listened to it ring as she walked to a back hallway of the restaurant.

"Hello?" Her father's voice sounded strained.

"Dad?" Liza attempted to control the anger in her voice.

"Liza? You're not calling from your phone."

"It's Sara's."

"What do you need?" He sounded even more distant than usual.

"Did you get my messages?"

"Yes, all of them."

"And?" Her heartbeat quickened.

"What?"

"Are you coming over to Pizza Palace?"

"No."

She placed her hand over her eyes. "Why not?"

"I can't."

"Why?"

"I'm too busy."

"You're always too busy." Her voice cracked.

"I need to go." She could hear the impatience in his voice.

"Why can't you come over for a few minutes?"

"I told you, I'm busy. I don't have time for this."

"You promised—"

"I can't talk to you right now."

Liza looked at the display on the phone. Her dad had hung up on her. She wasn't finished with the conversation and he'd hung up.

How could he treat her like this? She hadn't asked for much, only for a small amount of his time. Was it too much to expect her father to pay a little attention to her, especially tonight?

Now she'd irritated him enough that he'd hung up on her. Where did that leave her? What could she do?

She stared at the phone. He'd seen this phone number on his caller ID, so he probably wouldn't answer it again. She could borrow Tamika's phone and see if he'd answer. Of course, once he realized it was her, he'd be angry with her for calling him again. She shoved the phone in her pants pocket.

She could drive over to his office and see him face to face. From the tone of his voice, though, that would make things even worse.

She paced in the hallway, trying to figure out what to do next.

Why had he changed so much? Why did his career matter so much more than anything else? Didn't he realize he was hurting her? Of course he did. He knew, but he chose to ignore it. He'd been ignoring her ever since he became a partner at that law firm. She hated the law firm more now than ever before. Her pulse raced and disappointment coursed through her.

Though she didn't want to, she'd have to let things cool down and then try to talk to him a different time. For now, she needed to go to Sara's and somehow enjoy the celebration. After all, this was the night of a lifetime and she'd worked hard for it. She deserved to savor it without her dad ruining it. She was determined to have fun, no matter what.

She returned to the table.

"Who did you call?" Sara asked.

"Kyle?" Tamika asked with a giggle.

Chapter Three

"Girls, turn that music down. It's almost two in the morning and I'm exhausted. I have a hair appointment and a nail appointment before my meeting at the country club. I need my rest. I can't have puffy eyes," Sara's mother screeched from the top of the ornate wood staircase.

"Sorry, Mom. We'll be quieter." Sara crept across the floor on her tiptoes flashing a fiendish smile.

Liza lay on the brown leather couch with her head propped on her hand. The music played and her teammates danced around the room. Some of the girls displayed a bit more rhythm than others, but everyone laughed and enjoyed the dynamic beat. Liza wanted to lose herself in the music and think only of their victory. She'd spent far too much time worrying about her dad. Tonight she would party hard enough to drive him out of her thoughts.

Sara and Tamika approached the couch.

"I love this song," Tamika announced. She started singing into an imaginary microphone.

Sara covered her ears. "Make her stop. It sounds like some animal is dying."

Tamika slugged her in the arm. "I'm not that bad."

Liza coughed a few times.

"Let's dance," Sara said. She pulled Liza up.

Liza gyrated her hips and clapped to the beat. Sara raised her arms high above her head and bobbed her head from side to side while Tamika spun around and did a few punchy hip hop moves. Liza ran her fingers through her hair and let herself fall into the rhythm.

After a few more songs, Sara said, "Let's play Truth or Dare."

"We played that in elementary school," Brittany yelled out.

"C'mon, it'll be fun," Sara said.

Some of the girls sat on the couch, and others stretched out on the floor.

Sara started the game. She turned to Liza. "Truth or dare?"

Liza laced her fingers together. After some careful consideration of possible "truth" questions, she said, "Dare."

Sara tapped her finger to her lips. "Okay, okay. I know. I dare you to call Kyle Reynolds and tell him you think he's hot."

Tamika, Brittany, and the rest of the girls laughed and fell all over each other.

"I changed my mind," Liza said. "I want truth."

"Nope. You gotta call. You can use my phone." Sara rummaged through her pockets and glanced around the room. "Where is my phone?"

Liza had tried so hard to forget the phone call with her dad that she'd also forgotten she still had Sara's phone. She reached into the pocket of her pants and pulled it out. She stared at it. Disappointment and anger welled up inside as she recounted the phone call with her dad. Liza's face flushed, and her heart pounded louder than the music.

"Dial the phone," Brittany said in a loud voice while she twirled her short brown hair around her finger.

"Huh?"

"Call Kyle," Brittany said. She chomped on her gum and then blew an enormous bubble. Sara reached over and popped it.

Liza tried to focus on the request, but her thoughts returned to her dad. Once again, he'd missed something important in her life. Why? If he'd been in some accident and were lying in a hospital, calling for her, she could forgive him for missing her game. But she knew better. He'd skipped her game because he chose to. Her throat tightened, so she grabbed a can of soda and took a sip.

"Oh, come on. Do it," Tamika urged, clutching her chest and falling to the floor.

"No way. I'm not doin' that." She tossed the phone to Sara. "You have such a big mouth."

"Are you chicken?" Megan challenged. She clucked and fluttered her arms.

"Time's up . . . Give him a call." Tamika fashioned a serious look.

"No." Liza stood and marched over to the counter, her anger bubbling to the surface.

"What's with you?" Sara demanded.

"Nothing."

"She's mad that Kyle didn't ask her out at Pizza Palace," Tamika teased. She puckered up and kissed at the air.

"Yeah, that's it. That's the problem. You're so smart, Tamika. You've figured it all out." Liza didn't crack a smile.

"Chill. Tamika didn't mean anything," Sara said.

Liza stepped into the kitchen. "I know, I know. She never means anything she says."

"Why are you acting like this? What made you so mad all of a sudden?" Sara asked. She walked over to Liza.

"I gotta go." Liza pushed past Sara without even glancing at her.

"It's the middle of the night. You can't leave." Sara stepped close behind her.

Liza used her hands to emphasize her words as she said, "I'm not interested in any more games. I'm sick of it." She stomped over to the door.

Sara marched over to Liza. "You're acting really weird. Let's go to my room and we'll talk."

Liza backed away from Sara. "I don't want to talk to you or anyone else. I'm outta here."

Liza opened the leaded glass door and slammed it behind her.

Chapter Four

Liza turned up the radio as loud as she could. She ripped the hair band from her head, rolled down the window, and let the cool, moist air blow through her long hair. She didn't think about where she would drive. It didn't matter. She wanted to escape her disappointment in her father, and in herself. Her teammates hadn't deserved the treatment she'd given them—her frustration and anger had simply overwhelmed her and she'd taken it out on them.

She wanted to have fun at that party. She wanted to celebrate a victory she'd dreamed of her whole life. She wanted to forget about her invisible dad. Instead, he'd invaded her celebration by osmosis and ruined the party. How could she ever face her teammates after the way she'd acted? It was his fault. All of it.

Liza followed the unlit road as it wound around the ostentatious estates. Moonlight painted the rambling ranch houses, two-story stucco homes with tile roofs and park-like yards. For a moment, she considered pulling over, running across one of the manicured lawns to the miniature jockey statue that adorned it, and kicking it as far as she could. She shook her head. It wasn't the statue she wanted to kick.

The road veered left and right. The black denseness of the oak brush suffocated her, so she turned off at the entrance to the private beach. She glared at the locked gate, drove her car over to the side, and shut off the engine.

Liza inspected her car. It was an old, beat up VW Bug. The front seats were both split in spots and the ceiling lining hung down in places. A crack ran along the bottom of the windshield and yellow, oxidized paint covered the hood. Yet, she loved her car because she'd worked two jobs the summer before last to pay for it. It belonged to her and no one could take it away, not even her father.

This car provided her only connection to her real life—her past. Somehow, it bridged the gap between what she used to have and what she was now forced to accept. Liza smiled because it bothered her dad to have his daughter driving around town in such a "wreck." It violated his newfound image.

Memories swirled around and around until they swallowed her. She remembered, in exact detail, the home they left when her father coerced them into moving to Aldrich Heights this past summer. It was a small, three-bedroom tract house almost identical to all the others that lined the typical neighborhood street.

She closed her eyes and felt transported as she vividly recalled the kitchen where she'd spent so many rainy afternoons baking molasses cookies with her mom. She could almost smell the ginger scent as it wafted through the house while the cookies baked. Her dad would always say, "Molasses cookies? My fav-o-rite," as he walked in the house past the plain front door.

Even though the house was small and ordinary, plain and simple, it was a home, and in it they were a family. Money was sparse, but love was plentiful.

Every night after work she remembered how her dad would announce, "Anyone brave enough to take me on in basketball?" Liza jumped at the chance to shoot baskets with her dad. Night after night in their driveway, she developed a love for the game and a deeper love for her dad.

Almost two years ago, a large, successful law firm located thirty miles away offered him a partnership. She recalled how excitement punctuated his every sentence when he brought the news home. He told Liza how this would be such a wonderful opportunity and how it'd benefit their family. He talked about how this new partnership would make it possible for the family to take great vacations and do things they'd only dreamed of doing before. Liza was thrilled for her dad and proud of his success. Now though, in the chill of the early morning fog, she could only think how this success had spoiled him and driven a wedge between them.

The truth squeezed her heart. His career, not his family, had become his number one priority. Liza remembered the day he came home and said he'd found the "perfect" house, and they were moving. Liza didn't want to move. In fact, her dad was the only one who wanted it. He told them how important it was that he and his family present themselves in a particular way and that successful lawyers lived in certain types of houses. He also promised that eliminating the long commute each day would allow him more time with the family. Although they didn't want to leave their home, they all supported him in his decision. Now, sitting in the dark in her old VW, Liza regretted that support.

"I don't want to change high schools right before my senior year. I don't want to leave my friends or the team," Liza had told her father.

"This is a great opportunity for all of us. You'll make new friends, and you can still play basketball at the new high school. It's important for us to move. It's only thirty miles away," was his reply.

Even though the move wasn't that far away, it seemed like a foreign country, filled with unfamiliar faces, pretentious houses, and flashy cars.

Yes, success had changed her father. He spent so much time at the office that he regularly took a change of clothes and spent the night on his couch a couple of times a week.

Liza cradled her head in her hands. What happened to her dad? Her family? Was it too much to ask that her dad remember his family? Sadness smothered her.

She felt stuck in a place she didn't belong. She felt like an outsider. Her dad forced them to move and wanted them to pretend to be something they weren't.

That's why she loved her car so much. It didn't pretend to be anything but an old beat up VW Bug—no pretense about her car. If only it were the same with her dad.

Honk, honk . . . honk. The sound jolted Liza back into reality.

"You can't park here. Move on, please," a gruff voice shouted from the private security car behind her. Liza started the engine and drove away.

"Hello, all of you night owls. It's now four in the a.m. and I'm Late Night Lance here with you to rock the night away." Liza blasted the radio and kept driving.

Without realizing it, she found herself on Apple Grove Lane. She slowed as she passed the white house with green trim. She stopped for a moment. Did the family inside feel the same way about her house? Was it a home? She hoped if it was, that they'd never be forced to leave. She stepped on the gas.

Before she knew it, she ended up in front of San Silvers High, her old high school. She pulled into the parking lot adjacent to the gym. She studied the rectangular gray building and thought about the hours she'd practiced in that gym during the three years she'd attended. She remembered the first basket she scored as a freshman and how her dad jumped up in the stands and shouted, "That's my Liza. She's great." She could almost see him hugging her in the parking lot after her first game.

The memories poured in and suddenly they choked her. If only she could go back in time. She stomped on the gas. The tires screeched as her car bolted out of the parking lot.

Chapter Five

Liza stood in front of the pantry with a box of cereal in her hand. She heard her mother walk up behind her and felt her mother's hand on her shoulder. "Liza? Was there a problem at the party?"

Liza stepped away from her mom and said, "Nope. No problem. Why?" She ambled over to the white cupboard next to the sink, rummaged through it, and grabbed a bowl.

"I heard you come in early this morning. I didn't expect you until ten."

"I came home early, that's all." Liza poured milk over her cereal. She sat at the kitchen counter and faced away from her mother. She hoped her body language would communicate that she didn't want to talk to her mom about anything.

Her mother sat beside her. "I think something's bothering you. Why don't we talk?"

"I know . . . Why don't you leave me alone and let me eat my breakfast?" Liza didn't look up from her bowl.

"Liza." Her mother's loud voice surprised her.

"Seriously, though. I played the toughest game of my life last night and then I went to some lame party and now you're bugging me about it." Liza stared at her bowl.

"I want to help you." Her mother paused. "You know, I love you, even when you're acting this way."

"Acting 'this way'? What's that supposed to mean?" Liza slapped her hand on the counter.

"You're being rude to me and I don't deserve it."

"Well, if you'd leave me alone instead of annoying me with questions . . ."

A long silence hung in the air.

"It's your father, isn't it?"

"What?" The directness of her mom's question startled her.

"I know you're disappointed that he missed your game."

Liza looked away. She didn't want to talk about her dad.

"Liza?"

Liza didn't respond.

"Let's talk."

"I don't want to talk."

"Why not?"

"Leave me alone and let me eat my breakfast."

"Talking might make you feel better."

"Fine." Liza let out a breath and said, "Why should I be disappointed? I know from experience that depending on Dad to come to a championship game is too much to ask. After all, I'm not nearly as important as who killed who, or who is cheating which business, or whatever he does at his big, fancy office." Liza put a spoonful of cereal in her mouth hoping to conceal the fury building inside of her.

She watched from the corner of her eye as her mother stood and walked over to the sink. Liza kept her eyes on her bowl, but she could feel her mother's gaze. Her mom's voice was soft. "You really aren't being fair. Your father works hard for us. He spends all that time to make a better life for us."

Liza didn't speak. She watched the cereal flakes float in the milk.

"Liza?" Her mom stepped over to the counter where Liza sat.

Liza continued to ignore her. She'd heard this speech so many times. Her mother always defended her father. Liza chose to keep silent because her anger was so close to exploding she feared she might say something unforgivable to her mom.

"Liza? Will you answer me?" Her mom's voice quivered.

Liza still remained silent.

"You know, it's difficult to carry on a conversation with only one person doing the talking," her mom said and then sighed.

Liza muttered a reply under her breath.

"Excuse me? I couldn't hear what you said."

Finally, Liza's words shot out of her mouth like a cannonball. "You're always the one doing the talking on this subject. You don't care what I think or how I feel. You never listen to me. It's not like you're going to do anything anyway. You let him ignore me. What's the use? He's ruined everything and you let him do it. You're as bad as he is."

Liza couldn't look at her mother. She hadn't intended to wound her mom. It was her dad that she wanted to hurt.

Liza listened as her mom's footsteps faded up the stairs.

She stood, walked into the family room, and threw herself on the couch. She buried her face in the pillows. Now she'd upset, and more than likely alienated, her mother. She knew it wasn't her mother's fault. No, the blame lay squarely with her dad, but she'd said things to her mom that she didn't mean. Where did that leave her?

She'd have to make amends with her mom, but not now—not until she could figure out what to do about her shadow of a dad.

Chapter Six

Liza glanced at the clock on the microwave oven. It flashed 11:49 p.m. After their argument that morning, Liza spent the day avoiding her mother. She felt bad for the way she'd spoken to her mom. Sometimes, the words fell out of her mouth before she could stop them, and her mom seemed to be a casualty in the war with her dad. Day after day, Liza lost her battles to win his attention and her mom suffered the brunt of Liza's anger. It wasn't fair, but neither was the way her dad treated the family.

Her dad hadn't even been home yet this weekend. How could he blow her off over and over again? Her heartbeat sped up as she thought about her dad. He'd gone too far this time. He'd deserted her at the precise moment she most wanted him to be there, and she was determined to hold on to her anger until she could tell him exactly how she felt.

If only she could actually erase her dad from her life. Then the hurt would go away.

She turned off the lights, made her way to her bedroom, and forced herself to go to sleep.

Early Sunday afternoon, Liza spotted her mom sitting in the

sunroom, book in hand, gazing toward the sea. The soft ocean scent drifted through a slightly open window while classical music played in the background.

She slowly approached her mom, who seemed to be lost in thought. "Mom?"

Her mother blinked her eyes a few times, placed her hand over the book, and then turned to face Liza.

"I didn't mean . . . I'm so . . . It came out wrong."

Her mother outstretched her arms and Liza leapt into them. She buried her face in the curve of her mother's neck and recognized the familiar floral scent of her perfume.

Liza pulled back and wiped at her eyes. "I'm sorry, Mom. I don't know why I was so rude to you. I guess—"

"You were frustrated and I was an easy target."

"He makes me so mad. He's never home. He's never around. Ever since we moved here, he's been a different person."

"I know he wanted to come to the game."

"Woo hoo. Give him an award for dad of the year." Liza gazed at the ground.

"I'm sorry you're so upset. He's been working on a big case. He hasn't had much time for anything or anyone lately."

"I want to go back. I want our family back the way it used to be. I hate that law firm. I hate that he works all the time. I hate that he's deserted us for his career. He might as well be dead."

"You don't mean that."

"Maybe I do." Liza rubbed her eyes.

"You're upset."

Liza looked at her mom. "You think?"

Liza's mom sighed. She gazed at the book in her lap. After several minutes of silence she cleared her throat and said, "You're right. Something has to change."

Liza studied her mother. "What do you mean?"

"I've been passive for far too long." She patted the book in her lap. "I've been thinking about making some changes."

"You have?"

Liza noticed a tear roll down her mother's cheek. Suddenly

fear wound itself tightly around her, making it difficult to breathe. What kinds of changes?

"I can't keep living like this," her mother continued. "We really aren't a family anymore. His dedication to his career has pushed both you and Jason away, and I've tried so hard to compensate for it—pretend that everything is fine. But it's not. Truthfully, I'm not happy here either."

"You're not?"

Her mother turned her head as a flood of tears washed down her cheeks. For the first time, Liza felt her mom's despair. It clamped down on her chest, threatening to wring the last beat out of her heart. She'd never considered her mother's feelings about her dad's absence. She'd been so busy nurturing her own anger and resentment that she'd never stopped long enough to think about anyone but herself. Now her mother's anguish conjured up other thoughts. Scary thoughts. As she watched her mother silently sobbing, Liza feared that the very fabric of her family was disintegrating right before her. She reached over and touched her mother's hand.

"I'm sorry, Mom, I didn't think about how you were feeling. I thought you were fine. I guess I've only been thinking of myself."

"I didn't mean to break down like this. I guess it's been building up and I finally let everything go. I can't keep—" She wiped at her eyes with the sleeve of her gray shirt.

Liza's anger had now been replaced with fear and anxiety. Was her mother unhappy enough to consider divorcing her dad? It was one thing to be mad at him, but divorce certainly wasn't the answer. It was the worst possible solution. Her mom wouldn't actually leave her dad, would she?

Her mom snatched a tissue and blew her nose. She drew a deep breath and said, "I need to tell you something."

Chapter Seven

Liza's thoughts raced. What would her mom say? She cracked her knuckles nervously. Maybe she'd been too harsh about her dad. Maybe she should've kept her feelings to herself. Even if her dad was failing at the whole husband and father thing, she didn't want her parents to break up. She wanted her family to be the way it used to be, before her dad became a partner at the law firm and forced them to move. Maybe she'd set this all in motion by complaining about her dad. If she could figure out a way to make her mom happy, maybe her mom wouldn't consider divorce.

Sadness, regret, and fear all wrapped themselves around her as she held her breath and waited to hear her mother's next words.

Liza's mom caressed the book in her lap. She seemed preoccupied until she handed the book to Liza.

"What's this?"

Her mom sniffed and said, "Read the title."

"Book of Mormon?" Liza opened it and thumbed through the pages. She never, in a million years, would've expected her mom to hand her a Book of Mormon, but if it meant that her mom wasn't going to tell her she planned to divorce her dad, she would listen to anything her mom had to say.

"I've been reading it."

"Whose is it?"

"Mine."

"Huh?"

"I found it when I was going through some old boxes in the garage."

Liza wrinkled her forehead. "I don't get it."

Her mom retrieved the Book of Mormon from Liza. She cradled the book and said, "A long time ago, I was baptized a member of The Church of Jesus Christ of Latter-day Saints. I'm a Mormon."

"You're a . . . what?" Did Liza hear what she thought she heard? Her mind couldn't quite process the information. She blinked her eyes several times.

Her mother continued, "I was in college and my roommate, Sandy, always went to church. I started going with her, and then missionaries came over and I was baptized."

"Baptized? Missionaries? You're freaking me out." Liza swallowed hard. Her mom was a Mormon. The woman who'd been her mother all of her life was . . . a . . . Mormon. Never a word or hint or anything. A Mormon?

"It's been a long time since I've had any contact with the Church." Her mother sounded wistful.

"I can't believe I didn't know any of this. How could you keep it a secret?"

"I didn't mean to keep it secret. I didn't tell you, or Jason, because it never came up."

"Never came up? Seriously though, you should've made it come up. This is kind of a big thing. I can't believe you're a Mormon."

"I should've told you. I'm sorry I didn't." Her mom rested her hand on Liza's thigh.

Liza rubbed her temples as she attempted to digest her mom's revelation. "Why did you join, exactly?"

"Because I believed it was true."

Liza shook her head and closed her eyes. After a few moments, she opened her eyes and said, "What does that mean?"

Her mother placed her hand over her heart and said, "I knew it was true in here. When the missionaries asked me to be baptized, I knew it was the right thing to do. I know that sounds simple, but it's the only way I can explain it."

Liza felt torn between wanting to support her mother and fearing what this would mean to her family, especially to her dad. She decided to suspend her apprehension and try to keep an open mind. "What was it like to be baptized?"

"Like standing in a rain shower. It felt like I was completely washed clean. At that moment, I felt pure."

"And then?"

Her mom's face saddened. "My parents were so angry when they found out. They both screamed and yelled and then my mom cried. She must've cried for a solid week. It was terrible. It was like I'd committed a crime. I had no idea they'd react that way. I thought they'd be happy for me."

"Why were they so upset?"

"They'd heard horror stories about Mormons, and we had a neighbor that was a minister. He came over and wanted to cleanse me of my mistake. He offered to exorcise the devil out of me so I could be forgiven of my sin of becoming a Mormon. It was an awful time." She shook her head.

"What did you do?"

"I worked long hours that summer, and when I came home I went straight to my room. I wanted to share the joy I felt and I wanted to attend church, but I was too afraid of the arguments that'd follow. So I didn't. I figured I'd go back when I returned to college and was reunited with my roommate." She paused. "But when I got ready to go back, my parents refused to let me go and be influenced again, so they sent me to another college." She looked off into the distance.

"What happened then?"

Her mom brushed a tear from her cheek. "I didn't want to

upset my parents any more than I already had, so I went to the new school without a fight. I didn't know anyone. My new roommate was involved in another religion. I tried to attend church, but it was difficult to do it on my own. I did go a few times before I met your dad. I even attended a few times after we started dating."

"And he didn't like that, right? We've all heard him rant about religion."

"No, he didn't like it. He believes that organized religion takes away from true worship. I don't quite understand his thinking, but, when we started dating seriously, I stopped attending church because I wanted to please him. I was so deeply in love with him that I figured religion wasn't a big deal and we'd work it out later. As you know, that didn't ever happen."

"I wish you would've told me about this."

Her mom shrugged. "I've tried to push it aside. My parents were so distraught and your dad didn't want me involved, so I chose to keep the peace. When people from the Church would come by to visit I'd ask them to not come again." She paused. "Maybe I was wrong."

"Why?"

"Because, deep down, Liza, I still believe it's true. That feeling has never left me. I think I've been wrong all of these years to stay away from the Church. Your dad didn't want religion forced on you or Jason. He was so insistent that I didn't want to argue. I left it alone. Maybe the time has come . . ."

"To what?"

"Rediscover the Church."

"Are you serious?"

Her mom nodded and said, "I am."

Liza's heart skipped several beats as she considered her father's reaction to her mom's renewed interest in the Church. Wouldn't that drive a wedge between her parents and destroy any chance of finding what they'd once had as a family?

"I need to do something different with my life. I think what I've been missing is the Church."

Liza's eyes widened. She'd expected her mom to announce her plans to divorce her dad; she hadn't seen a religious transformation coming. She wanted to tell her mom to go ahead, yet she feared it'd make her dad so angry he'd be the one to consider divorce, and Liza's whole purpose was to not only prevent a divorce, but find a way to bring her family back together. "What are you planning to do?"

"I think I'll find a way to contact someone from the Church."

"I'm not sure this is a good idea right now."

"Why not?"

Liza knew how her father felt about religion and how volatile he was right now. She was afraid that if she encouraged her mom to pursue the Church, her father would flip out and things would be even worse; her family might be ripped apart permanently.

But her mom deserved to be happy. She'd suffered from her dad's absence and was entitled to some joy. Liza's thoughts vacillated back and forth. No matter how she tried, she couldn't come up with a good solution to bring her family back together. Of course, if her mom didn't find the happiness she needed, she might decide to leave her dad anyway, and where would that leave Liza?

Chapter Eight

Liza sat in English, wanting a break from thinking about her life, but her mind swirled uncontrollably.

She was still thrilled that her team had won the state championship, but the way she'd mistreated her teammates at Sara's party dampened her excitement. Her heart still ached as she thought about her dad and his disappearance from her life. What gave her the biggest brain cramp, though, was the idea of her mom being a Mormon. She'd never even seen that coming. How would her mom's religious reawakening affect Liza, and the family?

She couldn't solve all of her problems at once, so she concentrated on the one she could try to solve. Though she didn't want to explain her actions—especially since she didn't consider Sara, or any of her teammates, a close friend—she'd been rude and owed Sara an apology.

Once she apologized, she could stop thinking about what a jerk she'd been and give her mind a rest for a minute. Mr. Snyder's boring English class was a perfect time to fade into the crowd of students and think about nothing.

She stared at the back of Sara's head while she considered

what to say. Finally, she settled on the straightforward approach. She leaned up and whispered in Sara's ear, "Sorry about how I acted at your house."

"Is everything okay?" Sara asked.

"Yep. Stress from the game, I guess. Sorry. Did you get this assignment? I left my book—"

"Miss Compton, do you have a comment for the class?" Mr. Snyder barked as he sauntered over to Liza's desk.

"Um, no, sir. No comment." Liza heard giggles from her classmates.

Mr. Snyder was overly strict and often said that his English class was the most important class his students would ever take. He'd told them at the beginning of the semester that he accepted no late work and would not stand for any talking. He looked like a beagle, and when he glared through his half-glasses, he was cross-eyed.

"Have you forgotten rule number one, Miss Compton?" Mr. Snyder asked in his usual nasal tone. He held up his long, bony finger.

"No, sir. Rule number one: no talking in class," Liza said in a monotone voice.

"That is correct."

"But, seriously though, don't you think that's a little bit on the ridiculous side? I mean, you expect us to sit here and listen to everything you say and you never listen to a thing we have to say. You give us all these rules and . . ."

Gasps echoed through the classroom. Though no one liked Mr. Snyder, nobody ever dared say anything like this to him. He crinkled his long, narrow nose and locked his gaze on Liza. "Please, go on, Miss Compton." He let out a snort.

"Well, this class would be a lot better if you'd loosen up. You're too stiff all the time. There's life beyond this English class, you know. All you ever do is talk at us. We never get to say anything."

"Is that so?" Mr. Snyder crossed his arms in front of his chest.

Once again she'd spewed out words before she could think. True, Mr. Snyder embodied all of the traits that she despised about most of her classmates at Aldrich High. He was snobbish and rude and he didn't really care about his students; it was simply a show. He was like most of her neighbors: pretentious and fake. He wasn't at all like the teachers at her old high school.

But even if what she'd said was completely true, she didn't want to deal with the aftermath today. Why did her mouth always work so much faster than her brain?

Liza sunk in her seat. "I . . . I . . ."

"Finally at a loss for words? Perhaps we can now finish our lecture without any further outbursts. I expect you to visit with me after class."

Liza rested her head on her hand. So much for fading into the background of the class.

*　　*　　*

"What did old Snydie do?" Tamika asked with a grin.

"You should've heard her. She was great. She told him exactly what she thought. Everyone thinks she said it perfectly," Sara said. She flipped her hair behind her shoulders.

Tamika, with her mouth full of sandwich, said, "Come on, tell me exactly what you said."

"I'd rather have a little quiet time. I'm too tired to talk about anything." Liza laid her head back and let the sun shine on her face. She always liked eating lunch on the senior lawn because she could stretch out and relax while she ate, and today she needed the down time.

She continued to enjoy the late morning rays of sunshine when something unexpectedly blocked the light. Liza struggled to adjust her eyes and realized that someone stood in front of her.

"Hey, Liza."

Liza tugged at her shirt. "Kyle, how are you?" Silly question.

"I'm good." Kyle knelt next to Liza. His sky blue eyes sparkled.

Out of the corner of her eye, Liza could see Tamika elbow Sara. Tamika said, "We better get going. See you later, Liza."

"Okay." Liza gave a small wave.

Kyle turned to Liza. "I didn't mean to run off your friends."

"Oh, you didn't."

"I wanted to tell you again what a great game you played Friday night. It was spectacular."

"Thanks. I've been playing basketball forever."

"It shows." Kyle laughed. "I heard about your comments to Mr. Snyder."

"I don't know what I said or why I said it." Liza's cheeks warmed. She pulled her legs in to sit cross-legged as she searched her mind for something to say. "My mom's a Mormon." Once again, words gushed out like vomit.

Kyle smiled and said, "Really? Are you?"

"Oh, no, I'm not. She was baptized in college." Liza's voice cracked.

"Has she been to church?"

"Not in a long time, but I think she wants to go again, but she doesn't know when it starts or where it is or anything. You know, like that," Liza rambled on.

"Why don't you give me your address? I'll give it to my dad. He'll know what ward you live in."

Ward? What was that? "My address? Oh, it's 1215 Naranja Drive. It's over by the beach. It's not too far from school and, well, that's all." Liza bit her lip. Why did her brain have to disengage whenever Kyle was near?

Kyle finished writing on a small piece of paper. "I'll give this to my dad and then let you know. Okay?"

"Do you need my mom's name? It's Claire Compton or Mrs. Compton."

"I figured that."

Liza wanted to beat her head against the wall. Everything she said sounded so absurd.

Kyle stood. "I'll talk to you later."

"Bye."

Liza slapped her forehead. Coherent sentences seemed out of reach when she was within a mile of Kyle, and now she'd told him about her mom being a Mormon. What if someone contacted her mom? What if her dad found out? Why couldn't she keep her big mouth shut?

Chapter Nine

Liza and Jason walked into the kitchen. Liza had decided on the way home from school to keep her conversation with Kyle to herself. She didn't want to encourage her mom to rediscover the Church until she could be sure it wouldn't adversely affect her family situation.

"Hi, how was school today?" Liza's mom asked.

Liza sat at the counter and her mom handed her a glass of chocolate milk. "It was good," Liza said.

"Only because you were talking to Kyle Reynolds," Jason said in a falsetto voice.

"Kyle?" her mom questioned.

"Liza's been stalking him all year," Jason sang out.

"You're so annoying," Liza complained. She wanted to kill him for telling her mom about Kyle.

Jason grabbed a bag of chips from the cupboard and took off down the hall.

"Is that true?" her mother asked.

"Yes, it is. He's annoying all the time."

"That's not what I meant." Her mom gave her the look.

Liza gulped her chocolate milk. She didn't want to discuss Kyle or the Church. And the next time she saw Jason . . . The phone rang, interrupting her thoughts of beating her brother. Her mom answered the phone and handed it to Liza.

"Hello?" Liza said into the phone.

"Is this Liza Compton?" an unfamiliar male voice asked.

"Yes, this is Liza."

"My name is Steven Marcus. I watched your game Friday night. You played well."

"Thank you."

"Coach Anderson is a friend of mine, and he asked me to come watch you. He's talked about your talent quite a bit."

"Really? He's a great coach." Liza's face felt warm.

"I'll tell you why I'm calling. I recruit new players for Oak University, and I'd like to meet with you and your parents. Thursday evening, if possible." Liza gripped the phone tightly.

"I'm sure we're free on Thursday night." She glanced at her mom, who nodded.

"Can you meet me in my office at seven o'clock?" he asked in his deep voice.

"Yes. We can be there at seven." Liza again looked at her mother and shrugged. Her mom smiled and stepped closer to Liza.

"I'll see you then. Good-bye."

"Bye."

Liza pulled the phone from her ear and stared at it. Her hands shook as she hung up the phone. She jumped up and down a few times.

"Liza?" Her mom gazed at her.

"You won't believe this. I can hardly believe it. I'm in shock. I can't believe who was on the phone. He wants to see me Thursday night."

Liza's mom grabbed her by the shoulders. "Stop. Now take a breath."

Liza breathed in and out a few times. She placed her hands over her mouth.

"Slowly, tell me who was on the phone and what he wanted," her mother said.

Liza removed her hands and smiled. "It seems that Mr. Marcus, the man on the phone, recruits new players for Oak, and he happened to be at the game Friday night. He knows Coach Anderson, and Coach has been telling him about me." Liza stopped a moment to catch her breath.

"And?" her mom probed.

"He was impressed with my game and—get this—he wants to meet with me. Us." Liza couldn't contain her enthusiasm. She screamed and jumped in the air.

"Oh, honey, how exciting!" her mother exclaimed. She clapped her hands and smiled.

"We don't know anything, yet, but maybe I'll be playing for Oak next year. I wouldn't have to go far away. It's such a great school too. Everyone talks about it. Wow, playing for Oak. That'd be so awesome!"

Her mom grabbed the phone and walked into the other room.

Jason sauntered into the room. "Who was on the phone? Lover boy?" He made a face at Liza.

She glared at him and said, "I can't believe you told Mom about Kyle. You have such a big mouth, just like Sara." She turned quickly and walked to the doorway.

Jason shrugged. "That's what brothers are for."

"By the way, that phone call was from Mr. Marcus," Liza said over her shoulder.

"And he is?" Jason asked.

"The recruiter for the women's basketball team at Oak University."

"Serious?"

Liza turned around and faced Jason. "Yep."

"Why was he calling you?" Jason smirked.

"I'm not going to tell you. You'll have to read it in the paper when they sign me to play on Oak's team."

Her mom stepped into the room. "I talked to your dad. He

said to tell you he's sorry he's been so busy and he'll definitely mark the meeting at Oak on his calendar." She turned back toward the kitchen.

Liza and Jason exchanged glances. They both rolled their eyes.

Chapter Ten

Liza gathered her books and shut the locker door. Only one more boring class and school would be over for the day.

"Liza," someone shouted across the hallway.

Liza turned. She choked on her gum as Kyle made his way toward her.

"Hi, Kyle," she said, keeping her voice even.

"I gave your address to my dad. We only have two wards in Aldrich Heights, and you're in my ward."

"Oh." Ward. That word again. What did it mean? Not that it mattered much because whatever it was, she was in Kyle's.

"My dad wondered if your mom might let him come over to visit."

"Visit?"

"I told him your mom is a member of the Church, and he wants to meet her and invite her to church on Sunday."

"Oh."

"I'll come too." Kyle smiled.

Liza swallowed hard. Kyle Reynolds coming to her house? Whoa, that was too weird.

"Liza?"

Liza collected her thoughts and said, "When?"

"He usually makes visits on Tuesdays, but he'll call and make an appointment. Why don't you give me your phone number?"

Liza had to stop and think whether or not she had a phone number or even a phone, for that matter.

"Liza? Your number?"

"Oh, yeah. It's 576-2342."

Kyle wrote it on a piece of paper and put the paper in his shirt pocket. "Thanks. I'll see you later."

"Okay." Liza watched him run off to his class. The tardy bell rang, but ogling him was worth it. Yep, definitely worth the tardy slip.

Liza endured her last class by doodling on her notebook. Her mind wandered back to Kyle's impending visit. Her stomach flip-flopped as she thought of him sitting in her living room. What were the chances of her saying something embarrassing? Better than average. She bet herself she couldn't go for more than two minutes without saying something idiotic.

It suddenly occurred to her that she was in a precarious position. Her inability to have any sense of intelligence around Kyle had led her to agree to something she didn't really want. She rubbed her forehead. If only her brain functioned at half its capacity, she wouldn't be in this awkward position. She had to figure out how to tell her mom that Kyle and his dad planned to make a visit about the Church. She wasn't sure she even wanted her mother involved with the Church, and now she'd given Kyle her phone number and his dad would soon call to set up a visit.

How did she manage to get herself in this situation? Oh, yeah—Kyle. She'd have to figure out something before the end of the day.

* * *

On the drive home, Liza's thoughts shifted back to her dad and his obvious lack of interest in her life. Her anger began to build, and she decided it was time to talk to him. She couldn't keep waiting for him to make the move.

As soon as she walked into the house, she picked up the phone and dialed her dad's office number.

"Jackson, Samuels, Baker, and Goodman Law Office. Can you hold for a moment?" the female voice asked.

"Yes, I'll hold." Liza drummed her fingers on the counter while she waited for the receptionist.

After a couple of minutes the same voice said, "May I help you?"

"Yes. I'd like to talk to Jim Compton."

"I'm sorry, but Mr. Compton can't be disturbed," the woman said in a saccharin voice.

"I just want to talk to him for a minute."

"I'm sorry, but he's in a meeting."

"But I need to tell him something."

"As I said, he can't be disturbed. Can I take a message?" the woman asked in a condescending tone.

"I want to talk to him myself."

"I'm sorry, you'll have to call back later." Liza wanted to reach her hand through the phone line and choke the insincere voice out of this woman.

"Fine, I'll call later—a lot later." Liza slammed the phone on the counter.

"Who was that?" Jason asked as he rounded the corner into the kitchen. He rummaged through the cupboard for an after-school snack.

"Well, brainiac, who do you think it was?"

"Brainiac? Good one." Jason tossed his long bangs back and sat at the counter.

Liza covered her face and took several deep breaths. "You know, I am so tired of this. I've been trying to talk to Dad ever since my game. I've waited for him every night until I fall asleep. When I get up in the morning, he's gone. I've tried his cell but he never answers, so I decided I'd call him at his office today, and some rude secretary wouldn't put my call through.

It's so frustrating." Liza plopped down next to her brother.

Jason tossed a few crackers into his mouth and handed the box to Liza. He said nothing for a few minutes. Liza could see, from the corner of her eye, that Jason was staring at the floor. He raised his head and said, "Don't let it get to you."

"Don't you miss what our family used to be like?"

"I guess."

"Don't you want Dad to be the way he used to be? You know, before he made us move here and leave all of our friends and then he deserted us for his job."

"I guess."

Liza stared at Jason. "You guess?"

Jason shrugged.

"I had a long talk with Mom the other day. She's not very happy here. She wants to make some changes."

"So?"

"At first, I was afraid she was going to say she wanted to get a divorce."

"A divorce? Why?"

"Haven't you heard anything I've said?"

Jason shrugged again.

"Mom isn't happy. She's tired of dad's disappearing act too. But instead of saying she wanted to divorce him she told me—"

"What?"

Liza studied Jason. She bit her lip while she silently argued with herself. Should she tell Jason about her mom's confession?

Jason stared at her. "Are you going to say something or not?"

"Mom is a—"

"What?"

"A Mormon."

"A what?"

"Mom was baptized a Mormon."

Jason sat straight up.

"It shocked me too. She was baptized when she was in college, but Grandma and Grandpa were really mad about it. And then she met Dad. We all know he doesn't like religion, so she stopped going."

"Mom, a Mormon? Why didn't we know?"

"She said she didn't want to upset Grandma and Grandpa. And Dad."

"Weird. We've never done any church at all."

"I know. But I think Mom wants to go back."

"She does?"

"She's been reading a Book of Mormon and said she wants to contact someone from the Church."

Jason shook his head. He stood and walked out of the kitchen.

Chapter Eleven

Since the rude secretary had prevented Liza from speaking to her father on the phone, she had no choice but to wait for him in his home office and make him talk to her. She couldn't keep waiting for the right opportunity—she had to make the opportunity happen.

She ran her fingers along the cold, hard line of the large mahogany desk as she sat in her father's stiff leather chair. Light from the full moon seeped in through the parted drapes and illuminated the immaculate office. She observed the certificates and letters that hung on the wall. Each was neatly framed and squarely hung. The pencil sharpener, desk lamp, phone, and container of pencils were all aligned in perfect order on the desk. Two wingback chairs were placed at an angle slightly beyond the desk. The whole room was designed with her dad's career in mind—there wasn't a trace of their family in it.

She laid her head back and closed her eyes, imagining the scene bit by bit. Her dad would walk into the room and smile at her. He'd sincerely apologize for missing the game and beg for her forgiveness. Then she'd burst out of the chair and rush to him.

He'd give her such a bear hug she'd find it difficult to breathe. Together they'd sit on the small leather love seat and he'd listen to her as she described her championship game, especially the last few moments. He'd congratulate her, tell her how proud he was of her, and listen to her plans to meet with Mr. Marcus.

He'd promise to be at every game because he didn't want to miss his little girl playing for Oak University. To top it off, he'd tell her he planned to take a break from work and they'd spend it as a family vacation. Liza grinned as she envisioned the conversation.

The familiar ring of the phone interrupted her fantasy. She scrambled to answer the phone, hoping to intervene if it was Kyle's dad since she hadn't yet told her mom she'd given their phone number to Kyle. She picked up the phone and was surprised to hear her father say, "Hello?" It was wrong to listen to the conversation, but she couldn't replace the phone without notice, so she listened.

"Jim . . . are you there?" a deep, rough voice demanded.

"Yes, Bill."

"I've been trying to reach you on your cell phone."

"Oh. I must've left it at the office. I've had a lot on my—"

"Are you ready for the Scranton case?"

"I've been working night and day to prepare for it."

"Will that be enough?"

"Yes, I've been through all the files and I'm ready." Liza detected the uncertainty in her dad's voice.

"This is a big case, Jim. You need to win. This kind of a case can make or break a career, you know. Make sure you're ready for it. Nothing else can get in the way." It almost sounded like a threat.

"I know, I know. I've put everything else on hold, including my life. I even missed my daughter's championship game to get ready for this case. I don't know what else I can do," her father said, frustration evident in his voice.

"I don't mean to pressure you, but—"

"I know, my reputation is riding on this. You've told me."

"You're a good lawyer, Jim. Good night." The apparent compliment seemed cold.

Liza clutched the phone in her hand, listening to her father's labored breaths. He must have come in the house right when the phone rang. If only she'd gotten to him first.

He hung up the phone, so she did the same. His footsteps grew louder as he approached his office.

Liza didn't want her father to find her in his office. It wasn't time to confront him. Even though anger still clothed her tightly, she didn't want his mind elsewhere. She sat frozen in her father's office chair. She considered darting over to the closet or hiding under the desk, but he'd see her. She wasn't sure what to do so she held her breath and hoped he wouldn't open the door.

"Jim, is that you?" her mother asked.

"Yes, I need to get a file from my office. I'll be up in a minute."

Liza sat still, her heart beating wildly and beads of sweat forming on her forehead. What would she say when he caught her? The last thing she wanted was an ugly scene.

"Jim, can't you get the file in the morning? Please, come upstairs," her mom pleaded with her dad.

He opened the door, and the light from the hallway formed a narrow line on the light plush carpet. The door shut again, and Liza listened as her father's heavy footsteps disappeared up the stairs.

She exhaled as she waited a few minutes in his office. Even though her dad seemed to feel bad about missing her game, that wasn't enough. Not this time. Liza didn't want him to simply feel bad. She wanted him to change back to the dad she used to know.

Liza stared at the suffocating darkness. She rose from the chair and walked to the door. Listening to make sure that no one was in the hall, she opened the door and stepped out. The sight of Jason standing in the moonlit hallway startled her.

"What are you doing? You scared me to death," Liza said in a loud whisper.

"What's going on?" Jason stared down at her, waiting for a reply.

"I was waiting in Dad's office to talk to him. The phone rang and—"

"And what?"

"And I kinda listened in. I know it was wrong, but I couldn't help it." Liza lowered her eyes and pushed past Jason.

"What did you hear?"

"It was one of Dad's partners, I think," Liza said over her shoulder.

"And?" He followed Liza into the kitchen.

"He's putting the pressure on Dad to win this case he's been working on."

Liza slumped to the floor, and Jason plopped down next to her.

After a few moments, Liza said, "I guess that's why he missed my game." She let out a long sigh and placed her head in her hands. "Why do they have to make him work so much? I hate that law firm. I hate that he works there, and I hate living here. I wish he'd quit and we could go back . . ." Her sentence trailed off.

Chapter Twelve

Liza stood next to Sara.

"Do your cheeks hurt from all this smiling?" Sara asked through her clenched teeth.

"I had no idea it'd take so long to do these team pictures," Liza said. "I want to go home and sleep for a week."

"I think that'll do it," the tall man with a large belly said. "Proofs should be available next week." He began to disassemble the camera tripod.

Coach Anderson directed the girls to the bleachers. "Thank you for coming today to take photos. I think they'll turn out real nice, and we're sending a copy to the paper. If you'll indulge me, I'd like to take few minutes to talk about the game with Roosevelt High," Coach Anderson said.

"But, Coach, we won the game. What is there to talk about?" Brittany asked as she sat on the highly polished wood floor of the gym.

"Yeah, what's the point? We kicked their b-u-t-t-s," Tamika sang while she danced to imaginary music.

Coach Anderson grabbed a basketball. He took a shot. It

swished through the net. He let it bounce toward the door and turned to face the girls.

"You girls played so well against Roosevelt. I'm proud of all of you."

"We're number one," Tamika yelled out. She patted Brittany on the back.

"You know it!" Sara raised her right hand high above her head and snapped.

Tamika led the girls in a chorus of "We're number one."

"Okay, girls, can I have the floor back?" Coach Anderson asked.

"Sorry, Coach, it's too heavy," Sara said as she struggled next to the floor.

"Ha, ha," Brittany said.

"Now get ahold of yourselves," Coach Anderson said.

Sara started hugging herself while the girls giggled.

"I can see it's going to be interesting today." Coach Anderson sat on the bleachers until the girls finished goofing around.

"Okay, Coach, I think we can be serious now," Liza said. She gave a nod to the girls.

"Thank you. As I was saying about the game, you gals did a fabulous job, all of you. I was impressed with everyone, but one of you played extraordinarily well under pressure."

All the girls turned to Liza. Megan patted her on the back and said, "You were superb, Liza, no doubt about it."

"Yes, Liza didn't crack, and she kept her head even when she had the outcome of the game on her shoulders." Coach Anderson removed his glasses and cleared his throat. He looked at Liza with an intensity she didn't understand. "It's my pleasure to announce that she's been named to the all-star team for our league."

"I have?" Liza jerked her head back.

"I received a phone call this morning naming you to the team. Congratulations, Liza."

The girls clapped and congratulated her.

"Do you want to share your other news?" he asked Liza.

"What? What news?" Tamika asked with a smile.

Suddenly all of the blood rushed to Liza's face and she took a deep breath. His request confused her.

"Go on, Liza, tell the girls, I'm sure they'll be as excited as I was when I heard." Coach Anderson replaced his glasses.

"Ummm," Liza said.

Coach Anderson broke the silence, "You're too humble. Girls, Liza is meeting with Mr. Steven Marcus, the head recruiter for Oak University. Isn't that great?"

"Really?" Tamika asked.

"Uh, yeah. I have an appointment with him tomorrow night." Liza shrugged.

"That's awesome," Megan said as she tugged on her long red hair.

Lindsay, a tall, gangly teammate who sat the bench most of the season, said, "Congratulations, Liza. I wish I could play like you."

Tamika started dancing around Liza. "Good for you! Why didn't you tell us?"

She cleared her throat. "I guess I was too excited."

"You don't sound too excited," Sara said.

"If it was me, I'd be telling everyone who'd listen," Brittany said. She smoothed her short brown hair.

"I haven't had a lot of time to think about it." Liza cracked her knuckles.

"Are you going to play for Oak or what?" Tamika called out.

"I'm not sure. I don't even know what he's going to say yet." Coach Anderson had put her on the spot. Pressure on the court was one thing, but this kind of pressure was entirely different.

Coach Anderson broke in, "Since we've finished our team photos, why don't you girls do some layups at the other end of the gym and we'll call it a day? Please take your uniforms home and bring them back, clean, next week."

After the usual whining, all the girls fell into a line and ran to the top of the basketball key. They began the familiar exercises.

Coach Anderson walked over to Liza, who sat slumped over on the bench. "Liza?"

She didn't say anything; she hung her head a little lower.

Coach Anderson sat on the bench next to her. "I guess I jumped the gun. I'm sorry, Liza. I was thrilled when Mr. Marcus said he spoke to you, but I shouldn't have said anything to the team. Please accept my apology."

He didn't need to apologize. Coach Anderson had encouraged her and supported her throughout the year. He even scheduled a tutor for her when she struggled with algebra. He always had a smile on his face, and he never told her he didn't have time for her. She wanted to tell him everything that was going on in her life, but she decided to remain silent.

"It's okay, really. I'll be fine." She looked over at him and smiled.

"I'd like to believe you, but the truth is, I've been watching you wrestle with something lately, and I think I know what it is."

Liza untied and then retied her shoelace. She bit her lip.

"I've been around you enough to know what it means when you bite your lip."

Liza wiped at her mouth to hide her unconscious habit. "I don't know what you're talking about." She attempted to make her voice sound pleasant and cheerful.

"Come on, Liza, you can be honest with me."

He wasn't going to give up. It'd be a relief if she could talk to him. For a moment, she wished it were her father instead of her coach talking to her, but she realized that, at the moment, Coach Anderson was more like a dad than her own father.

"It's my dad." Liza felt a few inches taller with the admission.

"He hasn't been coming to your games. I didn't see him at the championship game."

"He was too busy."

The coach rubbed his chin and then glanced toward the girls practicing at the other end of the gym. "Sometimes, we men forget that it's our families that are most important. We get so involved in our careers that we forget where our hearts should lie."

"I've been waiting and waiting to tell him about my game and to make sure he'll come to the meeting with Mr. Marcus, but he hasn't been home much this week. He's been gone even more than usual."

"A big case?"

"I guess. He's always busy with one case or another. He used to be home and spend time with us." Liza wrinkled her nose and said, "Then he moved us to this place and . . ." Liza realized as soon as she said it that she didn't mean it the way it sounded, or did she?

"It's a lot different here in Aldrich Heights, isn't it?" Coach Anderson leaned forward.

"You can say that again. I don't feel like I fit in. You've been great, and the girls on the team are fine, but I still feel like an outsider, like I don't quite belong here."

"Except for basketball."

"Yep. Except for basketball." Her throat tightened.

"I knew the first time I watched you play that your heart was in it. The other girls all play hard and sometimes play well, but you're different. You have a determination that I haven't seen before. You're driven by something. I guess now I know what that is."

"What do you mean?" Liza cocked her head.

"You've been hoping that your father would take some notice. Each game you've played harder and each practice you've worked yourself more and more. You've practiced when you were sick and when you sprained your ankle some months back. I wanted to stop you, but I knew I couldn't. You were too determined."

He'd nailed it. One of the reasons she admired this man was because he never tried to conceal anything. He was honest and to the point. She sat on the bench and stared at her feet. She didn't know what to say.

"I'm sorry, Liza. I didn't mean to upset you." He sat back against the bench.

"You're right. I've worked so hard, and he's only been to two games this season. He didn't even make it to the most important game of my life. I'm just so—" Liza raised her hands in the air and shook her head.

"Disappointed?"

"Exactly. I hate his job, and I hate living here. I want to go back home where I belong and where we were a family. I want my old life and my real dad back."

"Liza?" Coach Anderson cleared his throat.

"Yes?"

"The one you need to talk to is—"

"I know. My dad. But he's never around. It's so frustrating."

"The only way you'll feel good again is to talk to him and resolve this as soon as possible."

"You're right. You know," Liza turned and looked at him, "your kids are really lucky."

"Why's that?" Coach Anderson asked with a smile.

"Because you're like a father should be."

"I'm not sure they'd agree. I've suffered from the same thing as your dad, only my passion has been coaching. I'm not sure I was always there for my own kids, but I've tried to make up for that with my players."

"Thank you." Liza stood. She turned and walked back toward the lockers. Coach Anderson was right. It was now or never.

Chapter Thirteen

Liza slowly pulled her car into the parking lot of her dad's office. She turned up the radio, leaned her head back, and listened to the rest of the song on the radio. She shut off the motor. Her VW Bug stood out in the lot filled with BMWs, Mercedes, Jaguars, and the silver Rolls Royce parked by the double entry doors.

She exited her car and opened the heavy, carved door. A whiff of cigarette smoke shocked her nose. She walked past two large potted plants and several blue-patterned upholstered chairs in the waiting area. Before she could turn down the corridor to her father's office, an impeccably dressed young woman called out to her.

"Excuse me, Miss, may I help you?" she twanged in a nasal tone that Liza recognized from her phone conversation the day before.

Liza eyed her up and down. This woman was definitely not Frieda, the regular secretary. This stranger was young and beautiful. Her hair was pulled into a ponytail in the back of her head and her makeup accentuated her deep brown eyes. The scent of expensive perfume hung in the air.

"I'm here to see Jim Compton," Liza said.

"Do you have an appointment?" the woman inquired. She crinkled her nose.

"No."

"Then, I'm sorry but you'll have to come back another time. Thank you for stopping by and have a good day." The sarcastic tone made Liza want to slap her.

"I don't think so. I know where his office is, thank you very much."

"Young woman, I'll call security if I need to."

"Go ahead. I don't know who you are, but I'm going to see my father."

"Oh, uh, I'm sorry. I didn't know Jim, I mean, Mr. Compton, had a daughter."

"Whatever, Mrs. . . ."

"It's Miss Jenkins." She extended her hand to shake Liza's, but Liza only glared at her. Miss Jenkins pulled her hand back and said, "Frieda has retired and I'm her replacement. I'm sorry we got off to a bad start. I was told not to let anyone past me and—"

"I'm going to see my dad." Liza walked down the hall.

"He's in a meeting right now. He won't be able to see you," Miss Jenkins called after her.

Liza stopped in front of her dad's door and stared at it for a few minutes. She wasn't sure what she'd say or how it'd all turn out, but she wanted to make sure he'd be at her meeting with Mr. Marcus, and she wanted to try to repair their damaged relationship. She was hopeful that once he saw her face to face and realized how important it was to her to work things out, he'd agree to talk and everything would return to normal.

She hesitated to interrupt him, but their family, and her upcoming meeting with Mr. Marcus, was important, more important than whatever her dad was doing behind the closed door.

She knocked. No one came to the door. She heard mumbled voices, but still no one came to the door. Again she knocked, three times. She waited. Her anger bubbled. True, her father had no way of knowing who was waiting on the other side of the door, but with every second her rage swelled.

She knocked harder. She put her ear to the door and could still hear the voices. No one seemed to notice her. Finally, she had no choice but to open the door herself. As she did so, she observed her father and three other men deeply involved in a discussion. They were all dressed in dark suits and stark white shirts. Her dad's tie was loosened, but the others' were not. Liza studied them and recalled the conversation she'd overheard on the telephone. She should be sympathetic to her dad and the pressure he was under, but enough was enough. She'd been more than patient.

"Liza?" her dad called out in surprise.

"Uh, Dad?"

He jumped out of his chair and, in a brisk pace, marched over to her. His dark, wavy hair was mussed, and he wasn't wearing his glasses. Liza searched his blue eyes, hoping to find something familiar, something comforting.

He pushed Liza into the hallway as he closed the door behind him. "What are you doing here?"

"I need to talk to you," she said with her jaw set in determination.

"I'm right in the middle of something. Can it wait until I get home?" He rested his hand on her shoulder. She straightened and he removed his hand.

"Yeah right. When will that be?"

"I can't talk to you right now. That's all I can say. I'll be home tonight." He stretched out his arm and grabbed the doorknob.

"No, Dad, I need to talk to you right now."

"Is something wrong with your mom? Jason?" He wiped at his face.

"No, they're fine. I—"

Her dad cut in. "Don't put me in this position. Those men in there . . . I need to get this case back on track. Court didn't go well today, and it won't look good if I take time for a family issue. Please, go home." Her father pleaded with her as he never had in the past.

"Don't you even care?"

"Of course I do, but I'm extremely busy right now. I must get back—"

Liza cut him off. Through squinted eyes she said, "You don't care. I've been waiting for you every night, but you're never home. I want to make sure—"

"I can't talk to you any more. I have to go back to my meeting." With that he turned around, opened the door, and ambled back into his office. He muttered an apology to the men inside as he shut the door.

She glared at the closed door as she tried to figure out what had happened. It hadn't gone well. No, not well at all. The gulf between them had widened to an ocean. All she wanted was for him to talk to her, work things out, and make sure he'd come to the meeting at Oak.

Why did he have to treat her this way? How would she ever put her family back together if she couldn't even convince her dad to talk to her? Liza struggled to control her anger while she considered her options.

She could open the door again and demand he speak with her. She tossed around that scenario for a moment and then realized she'd made a serious mistake by trying to confront him at work.

Liza shut her eyes for a moment to regain her composure before turning around and shuffling back down the corridor.

"I told you he had a meeting and couldn't be disturbed," Miss Jenkins said with one eyebrow raised and a jerk of her head.

Liza glared at her and pushed open the front door. She sprinted to her car and lunged inside. She hit the steering wheel with the palms of her hands. Not knowing what else to do, she started the engine and drove aimlessly.

Maybe she could go to the family cabin in the mountains behind Aldrich Heights. She'd be alone at the cabin and could try to figure a way out of this mess. She shook her head. Sharp curves and steep cliffs made traveling that road too daunting.

She could drive back to her old neighborhood and pretend she still lived there. No, she'd already tried that and it didn't help.

So she drove without any destination in mind for a while longer and somehow ended up at Aldrich Heights High. She stopped in a parking space beyond the gym and turned off the motor. A few cars dotted the parking lot.

Chapter Fourteen

Liza jogged to the school's gym, hoping she wouldn't see anyone. Inside the gym, the lights were on, but no one was on the floor or anywhere else. She let out a sigh of relief. Her footsteps echoed as she wandered to center court. She felt connected to the gym. It was here that she truly knew who she was. Outside these walls she wasn't sure of anything, but in here, she was Liza Compton, basketball player.

Without warning, a basketball rolled toward her.

"Hello? Is someone in here?" Her voice reverberated in the vast, empty room.

She snagged the ball and poised for a shot. She'd always dreamed of sinking the ball from the half-court mark at the end of a tied game. The ball glided through the air and, to her utter amazement, swooshed through the net.

"Wow, what a shot," said a voice from behind the bleachers.

"Who are you?" Liza tried to catch a glimpse of her admirer.

"You mean you don't recognize my voice? I'm hurt," Kyle said as he strolled out, hand to his chest.

"Funny. You scared me for a second. What're you doing here?" Liza exhaled.

Kyle darted over and snatched the ball. He dribbled it between his legs and then tossed it back to Liza.

"Do you always hang out in an abandoned gym?" Liza found herself intrigued. His smile made her forget why she was there.

"Only when I think I might meet someone like you here." He laughed.

Usually that kind of a statement would irritate her. She didn't have much use for all the lines she heard from guys. But Kyle was different. He seemed sincere and honest. "No, really, what are you doing here?"

"I had a meeting with Mr. Samson, the track coach. He wants me to run the mile, but I'm not sure. Boring stuff. How about a game of one-on-one?" Kyle rubbed his hands on his sweats and then clapped a few times.

Liza rotated the ball in her hands. She stared at the hoop. "One-on-one with you?"

"Come on, give me all you got, all-star."

She glanced at Kyle. "You know about that?"

"I heard a rumor. Pretty impressive . . . if it's true."

Liza grinned.

"First one to twenty-one wins." Kyle took a defensive stance.

Liza couldn't resist. She never backed away from a challenge.

She dribbled to her left and then to her right. Kyle was on her, anticipating her every move until she faked to the left and drove to the basket. The layup should've been easy to make, but Liza missed it. Kyle jumped up, grabbed the ball, and dribbled to half court.

He dribbled right, left, then right again. He took a jump shot from the top of the key, and the ball swooshed through the net.

Kyle seized the ball and threw it to Liza. "One–zip."

Liza's competitive nature accelerated into overdrive. She wasn't about to let anyone beat her at one-on-one. "I didn't think you played basketball."

"Not this year."

Liza played hard as she and Kyle continued their game. His

basketball tricks and attitude didn't impress her, but she reveled in the competition and the fact that he wasn't going to give her an easy victory.

After more than a dozen plays, the ball dropped through the net. Liza snatched it and threw a strong pass to Kyle. "Eighteen–seventeen my lead. Go for it, if you can." She cocked her head.

Kyle made the next three baskets.

Liza took her turn and dribbled under the basket using her left arm to make a reverse layup. She grabbed the ball and threw it to Kyle.

He paused for a moment and cradled the ball in his hands. He said, "Game point."

"What're you doing? Take your best shot. I'm ready." Liza crouched down, ready to pounce.

"I'm thinking that I'm in a great position here," Kyle said.

"What?" She stood and placed her hands on her hips.

"I'm about to win game point."

"Yeah right." Liza took her defensive stance again.

"How about if I make this next point you do something?"

"First of all, you're not winning this—"

"If I do, how about coming to a luau on Saturday? It's with our whole ward from church." Kyle grinned.

"Oh, come on."

"I'm serious. If I make this basket, you come to the luau."

"What if I win?"

Kyle raised his eyebrows. "That'll never happen. But on the off chance you do, I'll wear a grass skirt and do the hula at the luau. But you'll have to come to see me." He winked at her.

"Hmm, sounds good to me. You've got a deal." Liza bent down again, ready to steal the ball at the first available moment.

"Now keep your eyes on the ball, if you can. First you see it, now you don't." Kyle took off. Before Liza could even react, he made a shot from the three-point line.

"Aloha." Kyle wiggled his hips.

Liza squinted her eyes. "Lucky shot, that's all. Let's go to thirty."

"Nope. I won, you lost, and you're comin' to the luau. Come

on, it'll be fun. It's worth it to see some of the old men try to do the limbo." Kyle gave his best imitation and they both laughed.

"Saturday, five, Leadbetter Beach. Don't go back on the deal."

"Fine. I'll be there." Liza tried to conceal her smile.

"You can bring your family if you want, but make sure you're there." Kyle rolled the ball back under the bleachers.

They walked to the parking lot.

"We'll have the annual volleyball game too—men against boys," Kyle said.

"Now it all makes sense why you want my family there. You want Jason to be a ringer." Liza's eyes narrowed.

"Actually, I hadn't thought of that. He's pretty good, though. It wouldn't hurt."

"And what do I do while the volleyball thing's going on?" She cocked her head.

"You can be the cheerleader."

"Me? A cheerleader? I don't think so." Liza shook her head.

"Be sure to bring your grass skirt."

"I think I'm all out of those. I used to have three or four, but . . ." Liza laughed.

"Five o'clock, don't forget." Kyle reached his hand out and shook Liza's hand. "Good game. You lost, but good game."

Liza gave him a sarcastic smile. "You're so nice." Her heart skipped a beat. She couldn't understand why she felt so comfortable with a guy she'd only admired from afar. His blue eyes actually twinkled when he spoke, and he seemed so happy. She wanted to know more about him.

Kyle glanced at his watch. "Oh, I gotta go. Is this your car?"

"Yeah."

"Bugs are classics." He eyed the car.

"I like it."

Kyle reached over and opened the car door for Liza.

She jerked her head back and blinked her eyes several times. "Thanks."

"See you tomorrow. And at the luau on Saturday," Kyle said over his shoulder as he ran to his forest green SUV.

Chapter Fifteen

Liza drove into the circular driveway and shut off the engine. She knew if she saw her mother she'd be in trouble for being late, so she quietly walked around the back of the house and opened the door, hoping to sneak in without notice.

Her mother, dressed in salmon-colored silk pajamas, met her at the back door. "Liza! I have been sick with worry. Where on earth have you been?"

"I . . . um . . . I . . ."

"Come in this house immediately." Her mom followed closely behind her into the family room. Liza slumped on the beige leather couch. "I want an answer. Where have you been and why didn't you call me?"

"That's two answers," Liza said, hoping to lighten the mood.

"Not funny. I was so worried you'd had an accident or something. You were supposed to be home hours ago. I've been calling your cell phone over and over again."

"I must've left it in my locker. Sorry." Liza traced a pattern on the cushion.

"I'm waiting for an answer." Her mom's voice had an icy edge.

Liza wanted to avoid talking about her dad so she brightened and said, "I talked to Coach Anderson. He said I've been named to the all-star team for the league."

Her mother smiled. "That's wonderful. Congratulations. I'm proud of you."

"Thanks." Liza hoped this good news would avert any more questions from her mom.

"And that took you this long?" By the tone of her mother's voice, Liza knew her mom wasn't satisfied.

Liza considered what to say. She didn't want to argue with her mom about her dad. She also didn't want to make things worse between her parents. But she didn't want to lie to her mom and make things even worse for herself. After several moments she said quietly, "After I talked to the coach, I went to see Dad."

"At his office?" Her mother sat on the couch.

"Yes. But he couldn't see me." Liza could feel her mother's gaze searing a hole through her. "Some new secretary was rude to me. I wanted to make sure he'll be at our meeting with Mr. Marcus, but it was a bad time. I should've called. I'll talk to him tonight." Liza tried to act nonchalant so she wouldn't upset her mom.

Her mother was quiet. She cleared her throat, got up, and left the room. Liza threw herself against the back of the couch and pulled a large pillow over her face.

"Hey, Liza, what's goin' on?" Jason yelled across the room.

Liza said nothing. Suddenly, another pillow hit her head. She removed her pillow from her face.

"You are such a—"

"Raging pile of hot man body?" Jason rubbed his chest.

"Yeah, that's exactly what I was thinking." Liza rolled her eyes.

"Mom's been having a breakdown. She's called all over looking for you." Jason sat next to Liza.

"It doesn't matter."

"Let me guess, it has something to do with Dad."

Liza stared at her brother. He handled his feelings differently than she did. He distanced himself from their father and acted at times like he didn't even have a dad. He didn't let it get to him. She, on the other hand, let her resentment build until it exploded.

"I went to see him at his office. He wouldn't talk to me because—big surprise—he was too busy. He practically shoved me down the hall."

"Don't talk to him then." Jason shrugged.

"I can't just say nothing to him." Liza fingered the fringe on the edge of the pillow. "You know, I keep thinking our real dad is being held hostage somewhere and this guy is some robot replacement that's only programmed to work and ignore everything and everyone else. Dad wasn't always like this. It makes me so mad."

"Yeah, but that's life." Jason leaned his head back.

"No, it's not. I hate things this way."

"I thought it was Dad you hated."

Liza had to stop for a moment. She didn't actually hate her dad, did she? "I don't hate Dad." She sounded convincing.

"What're you gonna do?" Jason rose and walked over to the entertainment center. He snatched his iPod.

Liza sighed. "I don't know."

Chapter Sixteen

Liza glanced at the elaborate grandfather clock in the corner of the living room. "It's almost time to go. Where's Dad?" She cracked her knuckles and paced a few times.

"I'm sure he'll be here any minute. I talked to him earlier and he said he'd be home in time." Her mom caressed Liza's cheek.

"He better. After missing my game, he better make it for this meeting or—"

"Why am I going with you?" Jason interrupted as he walked into the room.

"I thought we could go out afterward and celebrate, as a family," Liza's mom replied.

"I've been thinking about this meeting ever since the phone call. I'm so excited. I'd love to play for Oak. I've always loved watching their games." Liza turned around and bent over to pick up her tennis shoes.

"Will there be hot women?" Jason asked.

"You're so lame," Liza said. She shot him a look.

"I wouldn't want to deny any of those college ladies a chance to go out with me." Jason strutted around the room with his chest puffed up.

"Oh, yeah, I forgot you're so hot every girl you meet wants to go out with you, right?" Liza giggled.

Liza's mom adjusted her blouse.

Jason examined himself in the mirror and combed his wavy hair. He grabbed his sketch pad and tucked it under his arm. "Where is Dad, anyway?" He left the room before his mom could answer.

"We're going to be late. Should we call Dad?" Liza glanced over at the clock again and bit her lip.

"Maybe I should leave him a note to meet us at Oak." Her mom reached into a drawer and pulled out a piece of paper and a pen.

Liza sighed.

The three of them entered the three-car garage and got into the brand-new blue BMW. Liza shut her door. Her father bought this fancy car to replace the old minivan they used to drive. She liked the car, but she didn't like that her father bought it for appearances. She resented it when her dad lectured her about how she should be acting this way or that way. He didn't used to do that. His whole attitude needed an adjustment, but for now, she simply wanted him to be with her when she spoke to Mr. Marcus. He wouldn't disappoint her again, would he?

They drove past the electronic gates and solar lights. As they passed the immense houses that lined her street, Liza recalled how much she missed her old neighborhood and how, only a year ago, she would have run from house to house telling each of her neighbors about her call from Mr. Marcus. Now, as she examined each of these mansions, she felt like she could never measure up to these rich people and their expectations. She didn't even want to try.

"What are you thinking about so hard, honey?" her mom asked.

"Nothing." Liza peered through her window.

"It seems like it must be a little more than nothing." Her mother reached over and patted Liza's leg.

"I wish . . ." Liza closed her eyes and laid her head back on the seat.

*   *   *

Liza scanned the campus of Oak University. It was spread over blocks and blocks of tree-lined streets. A new gymnasium was built a few years ago to replace the old one. It was a brown brick building with a glass-enclosed entrance. She noticed a few recently planted trees and some brightly colored flowers next to the entrance.

Liza had entertained thoughts of attending Oak but felt she'd have no chance with her grade point average. Yet, here she was in the parking lot, about to meet the head recruiter for the women's team. The possibility seemed within her grasp.

She dragged the brush through her hair one more time and ran her fingers through her bangs. She attempted to air out her shirt so it wouldn't be too wet under the arms.

"You look great, honey." Her mom reached over and massaged Liza's shoulder. "You'll do fine. Everything will work out. Have faith."

They strolled across the large paved parking lot and entered the three-story-high athletics building.

After they hiked up two flights of stairs and walked down a long hallway, they saw a door with a nameplate bearing the name Steven Marcus.

"Here it is, Liza. Good luck." Her mother turned to Jason, who was carrying his sketch pad. "Why don't you wait for us out here? You can work on one of your drawings for the art contest next week." She pointed toward a row of chairs.

Liza closed her eyes. A few seconds later, she opened them. "Okay . . . breathe." She knocked on the door.

"Come in," a deep voice said.

Liza and her mother entered the office. "Hello. I'm Liza Compton." Liza's voice caught in her throat so she coughed a couple of times.

Mr. Marcus stood and walked over to the women. "It's nice

to meet you face to face. You must be her mother?" Mr. Marcus smiled.

"Yes, it's nice to meet you." Liza's mom nodded her head.

Mr. Marcus stuck out his hand and gave each of them a firm yet gentle handshake. He pushed his wire-rimmed glasses up higher on his nose. "Please, have a seat"

"Thank you," Liza said. They sat in the burgundy-patterned upholstered chairs.

Mr. Marcus smoothed his thin, sandy-colored hair. He was clean-shaven, quite lean, and much taller than Liza.

"I've known Bobby, I mean, Coach Anderson, since we roomed together at Cal State. He and I played college ball. We both met our wives at the same dance and were married within a few months of each other. Our kids have grown up together and our grandkids are friends as well." He paused for a moment. "I'm telling you all of this because I want you to know that I trust his judgment. Ever since you joined his team this past year, he's raved about your talent and determination."

Liza's face flushed and she glanced at the floor. She pulled at her shirt and then looked directly at Mr. Marcus. "He's been great to me. Almost like a dad. That's really nice of him to talk to you."

"He believes that you and I can offer each other something. Are you interested in attending Oak University?" Mr. Marcus leaned forward in his chair.

"Yes, sir. I've thought about Oak for some time, even before we moved to Aldrich Heights." Liza kept her eyes on Mr. Marcus.

"And you, Mrs. Compton, would you like your daughter to attend Oak?" Mr. Marcus removed his glasses and gazed at Liza's mom.

"Yes. We'd love to have her stay near us, and we've always been impressed with Oak's reputation."

Liza's stomach churned. Thoughts of playing for Oak raced through her mind. It was unbelievable, incredible, amazing. A chance to play for Oak was a dream come true.

But where was her dad? She glanced at the clock on the wall opposite Mr. Marcus's desk.

"Am I keeping you from something?" Mr. Marcus asked. He replaced his glasses.

"Oh, no, sir. I'm sorry." Liza's face warmed.

Her mother spoke. "We left a note for my husband to meet us here. I know he'd want to talk to you."

"Would you like to wait for him?" Mr. Marcus sat back in his chair and leaned to the left.

"No, that's okay. He's probably tied up." Liza cleared her throat. He better be tied up, gagged, and left to die somewhere because no other excuse would do for missing this meeting.

"I'm sure it was something last minute. Why don't we continue?" Her mom smiled in that same familiar I'm-covering-for-your-dad way.

Mr. Marcus rubbed his chin. "I've been studying your stats. You're a consistent scorer. You average seventeen points and eight rebounds. You're also a strong defender in the post. I'm impressed that you won the free throw title at the Elks Club National Shoot-out. How many free throws did you make in a row?"

"Twenty-one," Liza said.

"Well, Liza, we'd like to recruit you to play for Oak. I know it's early, yet, and I'm sure other schools will be contacting you, but I'd like to sign you."

Liza cracked her knuckles.

"Coach Anderson has a lot of faith in your abilities, and from what I saw at the championship game, I think you have a natural talent that will take you a long way. I need someone with your skills, especially the ability to make free throws under such pressure. It won't be easy because we have a highly competitive league. I need players that can take the heat and still shine. I think you're that kind of player." Mr. Marcus smiled, exposing his straight teeth.

"Thank you." Excitement and fear filled Liza at the same time.

"I'm delighted to offer a local player a spot on our team. The athletics department also has a scholarship available. You could say that we want to sweeten this offer so you'll sign with us."

Liza's smile consumed her face as she considered his words.

"Mrs. Compton, I'd like to send some paperwork home for you to read. Can we meet again some time in the next few weeks?" Mr. Marcus stood and stepped over to a file cabinet.

"Yes. Thank you so much. It means a great deal to all of us that you have such confidence in Liza. She's loved basketball ever since she could walk and her father first taught her to dribble." Liza's mother stood and took the papers that Mr. Marcus handed her.

"That's evident," Mr. Marcus said.

Liza jumped up from her chair and wiped her sweaty palms on her pants.

"You don't have to make your decision right now. Please, go home and think about it. Discuss it with your family. Liza, I'd like you to stop by and meet Coach Blacke. He's been with our program for almost eleven years now. He's a good man and he knows the game. I think you'd enjoy playing for him. The women play in a couple of summer tournaments, so they're still practicing every afternoon until five," Mr. Marcus explained.

"Thank you." Liza felt giddy. She grinned at Mr. Marcus.

"Thank you for your time," Liza's mom said.

"Call my secretary. We'll set an appointment when you feel like you're ready to discuss the next step." Mr. Marcus shook Liza's hand and then her mother's. "Thank you for coming in with such short notice. I'm anxious to get a jump on my competition. I don't think I'll be sorry."

Chapter Seventeen

"My sister playing for Oak? That's pretty cool," Jason said from the backseat as they drove out of the parking lot.

Liza nodded. The idea of playing for Oak was almost too much to grasp. Her mind was in overdrive as she considered the conversation with Mr. Marcus.

"Are we going to go out and celebrate?" Jason asked.

"I don't know . . . I'm a little overwhelmed." Liza gazed out the window and watched the scenery pass by.

"Are you sure? This is very exciting," her mom said.

"Yeah, it is exciting—"

"But I'm starving. I thought I was going to get a meal out of this," Jason said.

"All you ever think about is food," Liza said. She laid her head back. As happy as she was about this offer, she couldn't help but feel her internal volcano rumbling. Her dad had done it again. He'd chosen work over her. Why was she surprised? She should be used to it by now, but every time it happened, it still felt like shards of glass imbedded in her chest.

Why did everything with her dad have to be so difficult,

especially when all of her basketball dreams were coming true?

* * *

Liza sat on the couch in the family room, still fuming about her dad's failure to appear at the meeting with Mr. Marcus.

"What's up?" Jason asked as he grabbed a bag of chips from the cupboard above the refrigerator.

"I've absolutely had it with Dad. This is so ridiculous. I'm going to wait, all night if I have to, to talk to him."

"Good luck." Jason sauntered out of the room with the bag of chips.

Liza stretched out across the couch and stared at the ceiling. Her eyelids slammed shut.

"Liza? It's late. You need to go to bed." Someone tugged at her arm.

Liza opened her eyes and yawned. "Mom. I'm awake, really. I only closed my eyes for a second. I want to talk to Dad. I'm going to wait here until he comes home, no matter how long it takes."

Her mom sat on the couch, and they both stared into space. Neither of them moved nor said a word for almost half an hour.

Her mom eventually broke the silence. "You never told me where you spent the rest of your time after you left your dad's office last night."

Despite her feelings about her dad, Liza smiled. "I drove back to school and went into the gym. I thought maybe I'd get in some practice time. All of a sudden, a ball comes rolling out of nowhere."

"How strange. Who was it?" Her mom turned to fully face Liza.

"Kyle."

"Hmm. Kyle again? Tell me what happened."

"He challenged me to a game of one-on-one." Liza giggled.

"And you won?"

Liza shook her head.

"You let him win?"

"No way. He was lucky, that's all."

"Then what?"

"Since I lost, he told me I had to go to this luau thing on Saturday night."

"Sounds like fun."

"Mom?"

"Yes?"

"I have a confession about Kyle."

"You do?"

Liza hesitated and then said, "I kind of gave him our phone number."

"To call you for a date?"

"Not exactly."

"Why then?"

"He's Mormon."

"I see."

"And I told him you are too."

"Oh."

"Was that bad? It fell out of my mouth before I could stop it. I'm sorry. I didn't mean to blurt it out to him. He makes me so nervous when I'm around him."

"That explains it."

"What?" Liza wrinkled her nose.

"A man by the name of David Reynolds left a message on the answering machine about coming over to visit. I didn't know who he was and thought he had the wrong number, so I never returned his call. Now it makes sense."

"I'm sorry, I should've told you—" The sound of the automatic garage door opening interrupted their conversation. Liza sat up straight. The muscles tightened in the back of her neck.

"Mom, can I talk to Dad . . . alone?" Liza implored.

"Yes. Remember that he loves you. He may have his priorities a little confused, but he loves you very much. I know that." Her mom gave her a pat on the arm, rose from the couch, and stepped through the doorway.

Liza cracked her knuckles and bit her lip. Her thoughts churned while she waited to face her dad. She wanted to yell at him for skipping the meeting at Oak. She wanted to scream at him for being such a jerk at his office. She wanted to rant about how he missed her game, and she wanted to tell him exactly what she thought about his failure as a father. But she still ached for him to be the father she'd once had. She still yearned for the way her family used to be. Somehow, if she remained calm, she believed he'd see her point, he'd agree, and they could work their way back to each other. If she started off their conversation with the good news about her offer, he'd be so proud he'd certainly listen to her other concerns. She determined to keep her anger and frustration under control and try to appeal to her dad to change.

She stood at the foot of the couch, waiting for her father's entrance.

The door opened and her father walked in. "Liza? Why are you still awake? It's late." Her father brushed past her and set his black leather briefcase on the counter. He removed his dark gray suit coat and threw it over the top of the briefcase.

"I want to talk to you, Dad."

He turned to her. "I'm sorry about yesterday at my office. I was involved in an important conference and I couldn't be disturbed. I have to get this case back on track. I—" He placed his hand on her shoulder for a moment, then walked toward his office.

"But I need to talk to you. Now," Liza demanded in a higher pitched voice.

He faced her and said, "It's late. Can't it wait until morning? I'm exhausted."

Liza's face warmed. She wanted to keep herself under control so she could avoid an ugly scene with her dad.

"Well, if it won't take long. Go ahead."

"Can you sit down for a minute?" Liza attempted to keep the mood light and upbeat.

He found one of the barstools and sat with his arms folded across his chest. "Okay, Liza, what is it?"

"You didn't show up for the meeting at Oak University."

"Must've slipped my—"

"Never mind." Liza waved her hand. "Are you ready for this?"

"Can you get on with it?"

Liza grinned. "Mr. Marcus offered me a place on Oak's team. He even said something about a scholarship. Isn't that great?" She bounced up and down a few times, sure he'd be so pleased he'd take her in his arms and apologize for everything. She'd have her dad back and they could be a real family again.

"You don't need a scholarship. Besides, I thought we agreed you'd be going to Cal State." He stood and walked over to the cupboard.

Liza's mouth fell open. Is that all he was going to say? She couldn't believe it. Her stomach was tied up in knots and her head pounded. She tried to control her pent-up rage, but it exploded.

"I can't believe you," she shouted.

Her father spun around. "What did you say?"

"I said, I can't believe you." She punctuated it with white-hot anger.

"Excuse me?" His eyes narrowed.

Liza said nothing. She recalled the words her mother spoke about her dad and his love, but she found it hard to believe he truly loved her. He wasn't the father she'd known. He was someone she no longer recognized.

"Explain yourself, young lady." He focused on Liza.

"I'll gladly explain." Liza placed her hands on her hips. "What possible reason did you have for missing my championship game last week?"

"I was working on an important case."

Liza shook her hands in the air. "That's always the excuse. You're always working, and when you *are* home, you're too tired for anything."

"Now wait a minute. I work hard for this family. I'm doing this for you so you can have—"

Liza cut him off. "It's not for me. It's for you—and you know it." She spat it out like molten lava.

"I don't think I deserve that at all."

"What about yesterday?"

"I apologized for that."

"You think a simple 'I'm sorry' can cover what you've done? I came to your office to talk to you and what do you do? You tell me to get lost, that you're too busy. You're always too busy. Now, when you finally come home and I tell you about my offer, you blow it off, like it's nothing. You don't even care." She glared at her father.

"What do you mean I don't care?" He took a few steps back.

Liza used her hands to accentuate her words. "You always put your job first, never us, and definitely never me. I'm sick of it. You're not my father. I don't know who you are, but you're not the father that used to love us and take time for us. All you worry about is money and what everything looks like." Liza wanted to hurt her father as much as he'd hurt her.

"I will not have you talk to me like this." He squarely faced Liza and pointed his finger at her.

"Don't worry about it. I'm done talking to you. In fact, I'm done with all of this. When my real father comes back, let me know." Liza ran from the kitchen to her bedroom.

She sat on the cold hardwood floor with her arms wrapped around her legs, too upset to cry. She fell over and lay on the floor, hoping to slip into a deep sleep where she could escape the sting of her dad's total disregard for her and their family, but she heard her mom's voice.

She tiptoed into the hallway and realized her parents were engaged in an intense discussion. It was wrong to eavesdrop, but she had to know what they were saying. She watched her parents from the shadows of the hall.

"You should've heard what she said to me. My own daughter making wild accusations. If she'd been in court, she'd have been accused of perjury. Lies, all lies." He pointed his finger in the air. "I can't believe she's turned out this way. I've given her everything she's wanted, moved her to this big, beautiful house. I even offered to buy her a new car to replace that pile of junk she drives around. What's the thanks I get? She accuses me of not caring about this family. Like I'm working for fun. How dare she say such things? She must be punished." He slammed the cupboard doors and pushed out a strong breath punctuated with a grunt.

She heard her mother ask, "Will we punish her for telling the truth?"

"What? The truth? What do you mean, the truth?" His voice was strained.

"Liza's right. You have changed. Your success has changed you in ways I never thought possible. You aren't the same man I married, and you aren't the same man that Liza and Jason knew only a few years ago. Success, whatever that is, has come between you and your family. Between us."

"What're you saying? I work hard for this family because I love you. I break my back day in and day out trying to get ahead, trying to make a mark, and you're telling me it's not good enough?"

"No. What I'm telling you is that you've lost sight of what's really important. You've become so obsessed with success and making money that you don't even realize you're sacrificing the only thing that matters."

"Which is?"

"Your family."

Silence hung over her parents like a soaked beach towel. Liza's stomach ached. She set this confrontation in motion. The last thing she wanted was her parents to fight and push her mom into leaving. She stood there in the darkened hallway, wanting to leave and not hear any more, but, somehow, her feet were glued to the floor.

"What are you telling me?" her father asked.

A few moments passed. Her mother said, "We can't live like this anymore. You aren't ever home. I keep trying to cover for you with the kids, but I can't do it any longer. You're never there for them. Or for me. It can't go on like this."

Liza watched her father pace back and forth. "You know, I'm getting a little tired of this. I work so hard and I do everything

I'm asked to do at the office. I spend long hours; I bend over backwards doing research and finding witnesses. And, all the while, I'm thinking that my family appreciates it and supports me."

"We do appreciate it, but you're missing the point."

"I work hard so we don't have to struggle to make ends meet like we did a few years ago. This partnership offered us the chance to get ahead. I want more for us, more for the kids. I thought moving to the city and working for a big, established law firm would let us enjoy success." He continued to pace. "You know how difficult it was for me when my dad died and I had to find employment to support my mother and myself. Even with all of my jobs, my mom and I went to bed hungry more than once. I determined long ago that I never wanted this family to ever be in that position. I vowed that I'd do whatever it took to not only prevent it, but also make sure that someday we enjoyed financial freedom. That someday is now. This partnership allows me to give our family success I'd only dreamed about before this offer."

"You're still missing the point."

"Which is?"

"The kids and I don't want financial success if it means losing our family to get there. We want what we used to have. We want that closeness, that family feeling. You remember, don't you?"

"Claire—"

"We miss you. You never make us a priority."

"Don't you understand that I work all of these hours and I do all of this because you and the kids are my priority? Why can't you see that?"

"Don't you understand that because you work so much, it's your career that's become your priority?"

"I don't see it that way."

"You haven't made it to one of Liza's games for the last several weeks. You didn't even make it to her championship game. Did you know that before she took her last free throw, she stopped and searched the stands for you?"

His voice lowered to almost a whisper. "I meant to be there."

"You always mean to be there, but that's not enough. Since

we moved here, you've continually put your cases ahead of our family. That's the whole problem."

"What do you expect me to do?"

Her mother seemed unusually calm through the entire discussion. "I don't expect you to do anything. It's time for me to do something." Her mother sounded tranquil.

"What do you mean?"

"I think we need some time away from each other."

"What?" Her father said in a shrill voice.

"For the past three months or so I've been thinking about making some changes."

"What kinds of changes?"

"It's not the right time to get into that."

"Why haven't you told me this before?"

"When? You tell me you'll be home and then call to say you have to stay later or you end up spending the night at the office. We haven't had any time together in months." Liza's mother raised her palms. "Did you think your absence at home wouldn't bother me or the kids?"

"You should have made me make time."

"You mean like Liza tried to do yesterday at your office?"

"That's not fair." Her father's voice was gruff.

"You were supposed to come with us to this meeting at Oak."

"I know—"

"You make promises you don't keep."

"But—"

"And I make excuses for you over and over again. I try to make the kids understand something I don't even understand myself. You told us this job would be a good thing for our family, and yet all it's done is tear us apart. I can't do it anymore." Liza heard her mother walk over to the cupboard, remove a glass, and fill it with ice.

"No. This isn't going to happen. My family will not fall apart. You will not do this. Claire? Do you hear me? I love you. You know that."

"Yes, I believe you do. But that's not enough—not anymore. I feel like you've transplanted me into an unfamiliar community and then abandoned me. It's like I'm a single mother."

Liza listened, hoping something would change. Finally, her father broke the silence. "I'll change. I will."

"Another promise you can't keep?"

"Give me another chance. I'll make it up to you and the kids. I love you. I've loved you for as long as I can remember. My life didn't start until I met you, and it'll end without you. Please, give me a chance to change."

Liza shut her eyes, sending a mental message to her mother to give her dad another chance so they could be a family again.

"I love you with all of my heart. I've never wanted anything else except to be a good wife and make you happy. I've tried, but it seems that I've lost you since we moved here. I don't know what else to do. I've tried to make things work. I've tried to deal with your career and be supportive. I so hoped you'd come to Liza's game and then to the meeting at Oak, but when you didn't show up to either one, it became crystal clear that your priorities have shifted. I can't go on like this; it's too painful."

Liza's cheeks stung as she listened to her mother utter what Liza had feared most. She couldn't hear another word. She turned around and shuffled back to her bedroom.

She lay on her bed. The heavy, dense darkness enveloped her. She replayed her confrontation with her father followed by her parents' explosive exchange. What could she do now? The damage was done and she wasn't sure how to fix it, if it could be fixed at all. Never had she visualized this. The relationship with her dad had gone from bad to worse, and now she feared her mother would leave her dad. How did it get so out of control? How did they get to this point? If only her dad meant what he said and would actually change back to the dad he used to be.

She needed to figure out how to get them back together and restore her family to what it once was.

Chapter Eighteen

Liza jammed books into her locker. She intended to race down the hall to get a jump on the traffic that squeezed out of the high school parking lot every day at three thirty.

"Hey, Liza."

She turned to see Kyle.

"So?" he said.

"So what?" She leaned against her locker door to shut it.

"You know, the luau. You did lose."

She hurried toward the upper parking lot. "Yeah, yeah. I let you win."

"Uh huh. Tomorrow night, then."

"I'll try."

"Where's the emergency?"

"Oh." Liza slowed her pace.

Kyle stepped ahead of her and walked backwards directly in front of her. "Come on, it'll be fun. Besides, you don't want to go back on the deal. Right?"

"Kyle, wait up." Liza knew it was Jessica screeching his name.

"You're being paged." Liza's voice had an edge to it.

Jessica caught up to the two of them.

"Liza, how's it goin'?" Jessica asked in a voice that sounded like fingernails scratching a chalkboard.

"Fine, thanks. You?" Liza forced a smile.

"Great." Jessica turned to Kyle. "I need to stop by Natalie's on the way home. Is that okay?"

"Sure. We can do that." Kyle stepped up next to Liza, who rushed toward the parking lot. "How about it?"

"Sounds like you'll be busy." Liza tried to appear unaffected by his conversation with Jessica.

Kyle grabbed Liza's arm. "Bring your family, it'll be fun."

"Thanks, I'll see. I've got to get going now, though. See you later."

"Bye, Liza," Jessica said in a saccharine tone.

Liza picked up her pace until she reached her car. Did Kyle think she didn't know he had a thing with Jessica? It was so obvious. Didn't matter, though, because she had a mission—to put her family back on track. She needed time to figure out a plan. Kyle would have to wait.

*   *   *

Liza gazed out the side window as she drove past the man-made pond inside the gates to her elite community. She pulled into the small parking area beside the pond, opened her door, and leaped out. She wasn't at all eager to go home and see her mom—or to face the effects of the conversation she'd overheard.

The sun's rays warmed her face. Clouds softly scattered across the light blue sky, and the scent of blooming flowers mixed with the moist sea air.

She scrutinized an immense stucco and brick home across the pond. A flawless archway adorned the entry to the front door and complemented the immaculate yard. A large and spacious Spanish-style house stood next to it. A silver Mercedes was parked in front of the three-car garage. She scanned each house that surrounded the pond. They were all similar in appearance.

Each house oozed wealth and status. Her thoughts turned to her father, and resentment seeped into her mind.

Bits and pieces of her parents' heated discussion flooded her brain. The word *divorce* shouted at her. No matter how her father had acted over the last year or so, she desperately wanted her family together. Divorce wasn't the answer. It was the furthest thing from the answer.

Liza snatched a rock and tossed it into the large dark green pond. Ripples radiated. She picked up another rock and threw it in. She tried different sized rocks and different throwing techniques, but no matter how hard she tried, she couldn't prevent the ripples that traveled across the pond.

She studied the water. Her life would be filled with similar ripples if her parents divorced. She shook her head.

Liza opened her car door and sat inside. She examined herself in the rearview mirror and smoothed her hair. She closed the door and started the motor.

Her thoughts tumbled in her head when she pulled into her driveway. What would her mother say? Would she still be in the house? Liza had snuck out earlier, before school, and had left a note saying she needed to be at school early. She didn't want to hear what her mother might say and hoped she could avoid her mom altogether.

Liza opened the car door and caught a glimpse of her mom at the large window that faced the driveway. She let out a long breath and hurried to think of how she could evade any conversation about her dad. Her mother met her at the door.

"Hi, Mom." Liza attempted to be cheerful.

"Hello, honey. How was your day at school?"

Liza slid past her mom and dropped her backpack on the marble entryway floor, next to the guest coat closet. Her mother shut the door, and the two of them walked into the kitchen.

"Where's your brother?"

Liza shrugged her shoulders. "I don't know. He said he was catching a ride home."

Liza walked to the cupboard and removed a large glass. She

stepped over to the refrigerator and grabbed a jug of milk. Her mother grasped the jar of chocolate powder and took a spoon from the drawer. She handed both the spoon and the jar to Liza so she could mix her favorite after-school snack.

Liza and her mom had engaged in many heart-to-heart discussions over the years while Liza sipped her chocolate milk. Today, though, Liza couldn't take the chance that the conversation might center on her mom and dad, so she dove right into her topic of choice.

"Kyle asked me about the luau again." She stirred her milk.

"I think he likes you." Her mom leaned over the counter.

"You're way off, Mom. He's always with this girl named Jessica. I'm sure they're together." Liza sat back on the stool and took a swig of her chocolate milk. "I don't know what it is about him, but he seems different than any other guy I've known. It's weird."

"I don't think it's weird. In fact, I think I know why." Her mom sat next to her. "One thing I noticed when I attended church so many years ago was the feeling I had around the people who were there. It was a kind of feeling I didn't have with my mom and dad. It seemed like so many of the people were genuinely happy. It's probably the same way with Kyle."

"I've had a crush on him ever since I started at Aldrich, but I didn't think he even knew I existed until he talked to me after the championship game."

"You're a beautiful girl, Liza." Her mother reached over and caressed Liza's long, wavy hair.

"Mom, really."

"You are. I've been trying to convince you of that for years."

"You have to say that."

Her mom shook her head. "No, I don't."

"Yeah, it's that mom rule that says you have to say nice stuff about your kids."

"I only speak the truth."

"Seriously, though, Kyle has the best smile. Maybe you're right about the church thing. He seems so happy. I've only spent a little time with him, but . . . " Liza shrugged.

Her mother leaned over and kissed her on the forehead. "I love you, Liza, more than you know. I'm thankful to be your mother, and no matter what happens, I'll always be your mom and I'll always love you."

Liza's throat tightened. She feared meeting her mother's gaze or asking her any questions.

"I've made a decision."

"About being Mormon again?" Liza asked, hoping it wasn't about her dad.

"Not yet. This is about your dad."

Liza felt light-headed. She wanted to stop her mom from talking.

"I think we need some time away from each other."

"He said he'd change." Liza knew as soon as the words left, that her mom would realize that she'd overheard her parents' argument.

Her mother gazed at her for a moment. "I think a break from each other will help us to both see things more clearly."

"But, Mom, this isn't what should happen. I know he's been gone a lot, but taking a break from each other?"

"I know this isn't what you wanted to hear and, honestly, it isn't what I'd hoped. We had some words last night and he left. I stayed awake all night trying to decide what was best. Your dad needs to figure out what's important, and until he does—if he ever does—I'm going to ask him to leave."

Tears filled Liza's eyes. Her worst fear was taking place right in front of her, and she was helpless to stop it.

"I know this will be difficult, but I think it's best, for now."

"Mom—"

The doorbell interrupted Liza.

Liza's mom walked to the front door and returned holding a long box.

"What is it?" Liza asked.

"A flower box."

"Flowers? Who'd be sending us flowers?" Liza wiped at her eyes.

Her mom opened the box and pulled out a dozen yellow long-stemmed roses. She gently touched a few of the buds.

"Here's a card," Liza said. She handed a small white envelope to her mom.

Her mother opened it. Her eyes glistened as she read the card. "What does it say? Who's it from?"

Her mother gathered the roses to her chest and closed her eyes. A tear trickled down her face.

Liza stood frozen. What should she do? What did the card say? Why was her mom crying?

After a few moments of silence, her mom found a vase and placed the roses in it. In a husky whisper she said, "Yellow roses are what I carried on our wedding day. They're my favorite." She arranged the roses and left the kitchen.

Liza stared at the small white envelope. What did it say? A little peek wouldn't actually be considered snooping, would it? She argued with herself. That card might determine her future. She had to read it. Her life depended on it.

She reached out to take the envelope but then drew back. Again, she reached out her hand but pulled it back. Finally, she snatched it and removed the card. She read its contents quickly.

Claire,

> *How can I begin to ask your forgiveness? I can't bear the thought of my life without you. I'll do anything. Please give me another chance. I'll change. You are everything to me. I don't want to lose you or our family. I've made reservations at the Stratmore Hotel for the weekend. Please meet me there tonight at six. My love always, Jim.*

Liza read it again. Could her dad have finally come to his senses? She couldn't contain her enthusiasm, yet she feared her mother had meant what she said. Would her mom give him another chance?

Chapter Nineteen

Liza softly climbed the stairs to her parents' bedroom. She found her mother kneeling at the side of her bed.

When her mom stood Liza said, "Mom? What were you doing?"

"Praying."

"Praying?"

"Yes. I haven't done much of it in my life, but I need some guidance. Since I've started reading the Book of Mormon again, I've felt an urge to communicate with God. Perhaps He can help me figure things out."

Liza didn't want her mother to know that she'd read the card, so she said, "Who are the roses from?"

"Your dad."

"Did he say anything on the card?"

"He wants me to meet him at the Stratmore."

"Will you?"

"I don't know. I felt pretty sure that we needed time away from each other."

"But isn't this a good sign that things might change? Maybe for all of us?"

Her mom shrugged.

"I think you should go. I think you should give him another chance."

"You do?"

"Sending you roses and inviting you to a hotel shows he's serious."

"Does it?"

"Mom, don't give up on Dad. Please, go meet him."

"I don't know."

"You still love Dad, right?"

"Yes, I do."

"You want us to be happy again, right?"

"Yes."

"Then go. I'll help you get ready."

Her mom inhaled deeply. She said nothing for a few minutes. "Okay. I'll go. And you'll help me?"

"Absolutely."

Liza marched over to her mother's closet and rummaged through the clothes. "You don't want to over-dress, but casual won't work either." She wanted to find the right combination that would take her father's breath away and make him realize how much he loved his wife.

She found a turquoise silk blouse. "This is perfect. It's dressy enough and will draw attention to your blue eyes." She grabbed a pair of sleek black pants. "I've got it." She handed both items to her mother. "You'll be gorgeous. I'll help you with your hair and makeup too. It'll be like a makeover."

"Should I be scared?" Her mother raised her eyebrows and opened her mouth wide.

"Mom, I'm an expert." Liza walked over to the jewelry case and searched through the necklaces. She pulled out a strand of pearls. "I've never seen you wear these."

Her mom rushed over and extended her hands. Liza handed the pearls to her mother, who handled the necklace as if it were made of fragile glass.

"These belonged to Grandma Compton. It was one of her few

prized possessions. Since she had no daughters, she gave them to me. They were handed down to her from her mother."

"I never knew that."

"I wore them on my wedding day. I haven't worn them much since because I'd feel terrible if anything ever happened to them. They're my only tangible connection to her. Someday, they'll be yours."

"Really?"

"Only after you can take care of them and understand their significance to me and to your grandmother."

"You should wear them tonight. Wouldn't that make Dad happy?"

Her mom nodded, and Liza helped secure the necklace around her mother's neck.

After her mom changed into the blouse and black pants, Liza motioned for her to sit at the vanity. Liza played with her mom's hair and used a curling iron to set curls all over her mom's head.

"I'm not sure about this hair-do."

"It looks fabulous. Remember, I'm an expert."

"I hope so."

"Now for your makeup. I haven't seen you wear any for a long time."

"I haven't felt much like it. But it's time for a change, right?"

Liza poked through her mother's makeup bag. "This is some kind of a color," Liza said. She held up some green eye shadow.

"I haven't gone through my makeup for a little while."

"Like a few decades."

"Very funny."

Liza did her best makeover job. "See the new you."

Her mom studied herself in the mirror.

"Perfect. You're beautiful." Liza smiled at her mom in the mirror. "Oh, one more thing."

Liza snatched a bottle from the top of her mother's dresser. She removed the lid and drew in a deep whiff of the familiar floral scent. She examined the bottle. *"Hope?* Perfect name for your signature perfume." Liza spritzed her mom a few times. "This perfume always reminds me of you. Somehow, whenever I smell it, I feel safe and secure because it makes me think you're somewhere near."

Her mother stood and embraced Liza. "Thank you. I think this may be a turning point for us."

"I'm going to keep my fingers and toes, arms, legs, and everything else crossed, even my eyes. See?" Liza said with eyes crossed.

"You know, your eyes might stay that way." Her mom laughed. With a more serious tone she asked, "Before I leave, tell me how you feel about your dad."

Liza remained quiet for a few minutes while she considered her feelings. She glanced at her mother. "I'm still mad and disappointed, but I think if you and Dad work through things, then Dad and I can too."

"Good."

A warm feeling encompassed Liza. Maybe they'd be a family again after all.

Chapter Twenty

Jason strolled over to the breakfast bar and sat on the bar-stool. He balanced himself as he placed his feet on the counter and leaned back.

"What're you doing? Take your feet off the counter." Liza pushed his size fifteen feet off the edge. Jason caught himself so he didn't fall to the floor.

"What's with you today, Queen Liza?"

Liza sat next to her brother.

"Don't tell me the queen is going to address her subject," he said in an English accent. He bowed his head.

"If you can be mature for a small moment, I have something to tell you."

"What's the big news?" He accentuated each word.

Liza studied Jason and shook her head. She argued with herself. Finally, she said, "Mom and Dad are at a hotel for the weekend."

"Yeah, I know, Mom left a message on my phone."

"Oh . . . Well, this is a good thing."

"Why?"

"Are you completely oblivious?"

"No."

"Do you even know what 'oblivious' means?"

"I—"

"Never mind." Liza sighed.

"Whatever." Jason shrugged and leaned back on the stool with his feet on the counter again.

Liza rubbed her forehead. "You're so lame."

The phone started ringing. "Must be my fans," Jason said as he lunged for the handset. "I've been expecting a call."

"Hey, beautiful . . . oh, yeah. Sorry, dude. Here she is . . . I guess it's for you." Jason handed Liza the phone.

"Hello?"

"Hi, it's Kyle."

Liza swallowed hard and said, "Hi."

"I'm calling to remind you about the luau. You and your family are coming, right?"

"Well—" she started.

"Now don't be giving me any excuses. You lost, so now you need to make good on our agreement and come to the luau." She knew he was grinning.

"I'm not trying to get out of it, but my mom and dad are away for the weekend."

"You and Jason can still come."

"I don't know—"

"I won't take no for an answer. I even have a grass skirt for you."

"I never agreed to wear a grass skirt."

Jason started doing the hula in front of Liza, so she turned her back on him.

"Do you want me to pick you up?" Kyle asked.

Jason stepped in front of her and made faces. He kissed the air. She fluttered her eyelashes. "No, that's okay. I'll meet you over there, I guess."

"You're sure?"

"Yeah."

"I'll see you about five o'clock then."

"Okay. Bye." She clutched the phone to her chest.

"Oooo, it was Kyle," Jason said in a falsetto voice as he poked Liza.

"One of these days, Jason. One of these days." She punched the air with her fist.

"I'm shaking with fear." Jason shook his body erratically. "What'd he want, anyway? And what about a grass skirt?"

"He's invited us to a luau thing at Leadbetter Beach."

"A what?" Jason took a few steps back.

"It's a long story. Kyle said there'd be food, hula dancing, and even a volleyball game."

"Hmm. Volleyball, huh? And food? Two of my favorites." Jason rubbed his hands together.

"I'm sure there'll be some girls too."

Jason shrugged. "I'm in."

*   *   *

Liza braided her hair and secured it with a rubber band. She checked her makeup and fiddled with her shirt. She tucked it in, pulled it out, tucked it in again, and pulled it out. She inspected herself in the mirror and determined she was in serious need of a tan.

"Hey, Jason, are you ready? It's already five ten," she yelled while she walked down the hall toward the family room.

"Chill out," Jason yelled back.

After a few minutes, Jason bounded into the family room.

Liza gave him a look and said, "It started at five. What's the problem?"

"Colin called and I'm going to catch a movie with him, and then Ian's having a party."

"What? No way. I mean, it's pathetic enough showing up with my brother, but by myself? I'll feel so lame. Please, come with me."

"Colin's on his way over."

"Jason. You said you'd go."

"Kyle will keep you company." He patted her on the back.

"You're such a loser." She shook her head.

A horn sounded.

"There's Colin. See ya. Try to keep your drooling to a minimum." Jason laughed as he walked out the front door.

Liza clenched her fists and let out a shriek. How could she possibly go to the luau by herself? She'd seem pitiful. Why did Jason have to be such a loser anyway? The more she thought about him, the madder it made her. Finally, she grabbed a pillow and hurled it at the front door. She stomped out of the family room and threw the door open to the garage.

She sat in her car. There was no way she could go by herself. Everyone would know she only came to see Kyle. She'd look like a stalker.

Going anywhere alone was social death. Maybe she could secretly drive past. No, he knew her car, and then she'd feel like an even bigger dork. If only Jason hadn't baled on her.

She got out of the car. She got back in. She got out. In. Out. In. *Ridiculous. It's just a party. No big deal. Go, act casual, and see what happens.* After all, Kyle *had* called to remind her. Maybe he really wanted her to come. Was it possible that he liked her even though she wasn't Mormon? What about Jessica?

She sat in the car a few more minutes. Pretty soon it'd be too late to go, so she had to decide one way or the other. She took a deep breath and started the engine.

As she pulled into the parking lot at the beach, she spotted the group immediately. She parked in a space and, for a moment, sat in the car trying to breathe normally. Her heart raced and she had to wipe her moist palms on the seat cover.

Her door whipped open.

Chapter Twenty-One

"I thought you weren't going to make it." Kyle stood there with a grin that could light up a small city.

"Jason backed out at the last minute, and I wasn't sure about coming by myself."

Kyle reached his hand out and pulled Liza to her feet. "Come on over. We're about to start eating. Then we'll have the big volleyball game. Too bad about Jason. I was hoping he'd win the game for us. I'm not much of a volleyball player. Basketball's really my game." He winked.

They walked over to the crowded picnic tables.

"Hi, Liza," Jessica said.

"Hi."

"Hey, Liza," Natalie said.

"Hi."

Kyle guided Liza to a table under a tall palm tree. "This is my dad. And this is my mom."

"Hello, nice to meet you, Liza," Kyle's mother said. She didn't resemble Kyle, though she was tall and had blue eyes.

"We're glad you came. I'm hoping to visit your family next

week," Mr. Reynolds said in a kind voice. Kyle was almost an exact replica of his father.

Liza bit her lip.

"Why don't you two get in line?" Mrs. Reynolds suggested.

"Okay." Liza watched as everyone bowed their heads in unison. She couldn't quite hear what a man said up front, but she heard everyone say amen at the conclusion of his words.

"This is great food. Do you do this a lot?" Liza filled her plate with fresh fruit and roasted pork. She followed Kyle back to the table and sat down.

"We have dinners every now and then. We have this luau every year. It's kind of a tradition," Kyle said. "It's to welcome spring, or something like that."

"I can't believe how many little kids are here." Liza surveyed the crowd.

"We have seven kids in our family."

"Seriously?"

"Three of them are in college, one brother's in South America on a mission for the Church, and my oldest sister is married and lives in Oregon."

"I can't imagine having that many in my family. One brother is quite enough, thanks."

"It's actually pretty cool. We have fun together. Dad likes to take us fishing on the boat. We go camping every summer too. I guess I've never thought of us as being different."

"Sounds fun. My family isn't much like that."

"Tell me about your family."

"Not much to tell. We moved here last summer and that's about it." Liza shrugged. She bit into a piece of fresh pineapple. "This is so good. I love pineapple." Afraid she'd do something embarrassing, like drool pineapple juice down her chin, she reached for a napkin. Kyle reached for one at the same time. As soon as his hand touched hers, a flock of butterflies materialized in her stomach.

Jessica interrupted, "Kyle, we need you at the volleyball court. I'm sure Liza can spare you, isn't that right?"

"Give me a minute, Jess," Kyle said.

"No, really, the game's about to start and you've wasted enough time eating and stuff." She glared at Liza.

"Come on, Liza," Kyle said.

"Oh, she'll be fine here. Won't you?" Jessica smiled.

Liza gave an equally insincere smile. "Sure. No problem, Jessica."

Liza watched Jessica and Kyle walk to the sand volleyball court. She wanted to run over, tackle Jessica to the ground, and rub her smug face in the gritty sand.

Liza felt someone standing behind her. "You're Liza Compton, right?" Liza turned to see a girl a few years younger than herself sit on the bench next to her.

"Yeah, that's me."

"I'm Cassie. I've seen you play basketball. You're awesome." Cassie played with her dirty-blonde, shoulder-length hair.

"Thanks."

"I play in the orchestra. The viola. It's a little bigger than a violin. It's not as cool as playing basketball." Cassie fingered her glasses and looked down at her feet.

"I think playing an instrument is great. I don't play one at all. Never have. I've only known basketball. I guess it's my thing."

"You're sure good at it. Everyone talks about how different the team is this year with you. And winning the championship must have been so awesome."

"Yep, pretty amazing," Liza said. She glanced over at the volleyball court and saw Jessica hanging all over Kyle.

"She does that all the time," Cassie said.

"What?"

"Jess. She loves to flirt with Kyle. I don't think he likes her, though. He's not going out with anyone. You know, mission prep."

"Mission prep?"

"He's going on his mission in the fall, I think. My brother went to Australia on his mission, and he had a girlfriend he met at college. Bad news. At least that's what my parents said. He's going to be home in about a month and his old girlfriend got married six months ago."

"Okay." Liza's eyes grew a little bigger.

"Jess has had a crush on Kyle for like forever. I hear about it all the time. She's always talking about him and making hearts on her notebooks. She says she's gonna wait for him while he goes on his mission."

"Really."

"Oh, yeah."

"I think she's pretty obnoxious, myself." Liza snickered.

"Yeah, she's been like that forever too."

"How long have you known her?" Liza asked coolly.

"Pretty much all my life." Cassie paused a moment, "She's my sister."

"Sister?" Liza's face flushed. Why did she did she always have to blurt things out before her brain was in gear?

"Don't worry. She can be nice, sometimes. Kyle, he's usually nice. All the girls in our ward have had crushes on him. I think that's kind of made him think he's pretty hot."

"Is that so?"

"Are you coming to church?" Cassie cocked her head to the side.

"Um, I don't know. Kyle invited me to this, and I thought I'd come check it out. I've never been to a church. My dad's not into religion."

"You're not Mormon?"

"No."

"Oh. I thought maybe you were a member but hadn't come to church, yet, or something. Are you going to come anyway?"

"You ask a lot of questions."

"I know. Jess tells me I'm really annoying, but I think I'm curious."

"We should go over by the game so we can see it." Liza stood and briskly walked to the sand court with Cassie close behind.

Liza and Cassie sat on the grass knoll a few feet from the

court. Liza watched the game, though most of her attention centered on Kyle. He was beautiful, no doubt about it. If he wasn't interested in Jessica, as Cassie said, maybe she had a chance with him. Or not. A mission?

"Team point," a large man yelled from the sideline.

Kyle served the ball. The men's team volleyed it a few times and Kyle's dad jumped up to spike it—right into the net.

"Way to go, Dad." Kyle ran over and slapped his dad on the back.

"If only that net hadn't moved right when I spiked it," his dad said.

"Yeah, yeah, that's what you say every year." Kyle wiped at his shorts.

"Hey, last year we beat you boys." Mr. Reynolds reached his arm around Kyle.

"Pure luck."

"Athletic prowess, you mean." Mr. Reynolds pulled his sleeve up a bit and flexed his biceps. Both teams broke out in laughter.

Liza joined in, but she found herself jealous of Kyle's relationship with his dad.

Kyle ran over and planted himself next to Liza. "What'd you think?"

"Your dad has big muscles." Liza giggled.

"No, I mean me."

"You were alright."

Kyle grinned.

Jessica ran up. "Oh, Kyle, you were so good in the game. You're always the best. How about getting some dessert? My mom made her yummy cheesecake." Jessica leaned in toward Kyle, ignoring Liza.

"Thanks, but I'm going to hang out here for a minute."

"I'll save you a slice, and a seat right next to me." She gave Liza the glare of death. "Come on, Cassie." Jessica smiled at Kyle. Cassie stood and followed her sister.

Liza watched Jessica saunter over to the dessert table. "You can get dessert if you want."

"Naw. I'd rather race you to the ocean." With that, Kyle jumped to his feet and darted toward the water.

Liza's competitive streak kicked in. She hit the ground running, trying to overtake Kyle before reaching the soft, gushy sand.

Chapter Twenty-Two

"Let's swim," Kyle said.

"No way. The water's freezing." Liza held her hands up in front of her.

"Chicken." Kyle clucked a few times.

"No, I'd call it intelligence."

"Oh, come on. It'll be fun."

"Thanks, but I'd rather stay dry. No swimming for me."

Kyle stepped over and wrapped his arms around Liza. For a moment, she thought her heart dropped out of her body and fell on the sand. She melted into his grasp.

"What if I toss you in the water?" he whispered into her ear.

"You wouldn't dare," Liza said.

"I don't know. A dare? I love dares."

"No, really, I don't want to get wet."

Kyle pulled her toward the water. Her feet dragged along the wet sand, leaving two ruts.

"Kyle, I mean it." She tried to voice her determination.

Still he continued toward the water. Liza squirmed. Kyle picked her up and continued. She struggled harder.

"Kyle, if you dunk me, I'll be so mad at you."

Still he trudged on toward the ocean.

The cold, wet sensation shocked her feet, her shins, her knees, and the bottom of her thighs. The chill of the water left her breathless.

"Kyle, really, I'll scream," she said in a high-pitched voice.

Finally, he let go and Liza fell a little deeper into the water.

"I'm freezing." She cupped her hand and splashed him. He returned the favor and soon they were both sopping wet.

Liza shook her hands and pulled the drenched sweatshirt from her body. She looked at Kyle. He reminded her of a wet dog. She started laughing.

"What's so funny?" he said.

Liza continued to laugh. He splashed her and she splashed back. Soon they were both laughing and dripping wet, again.

"Kyle, what are you two doing?"

Liza jerked around and saw Jessica standing at the edge of the water.

"Oh, us? We're . . ." Kyle let his sentence trail off.

Liza giggled.

Jessica spun on her heels and stomped away.

"Uh oh. I think we made your girlfriend mad," Liza said, wiping at her face.

"Jess? Girlfriend?" He laughed. "We're friends, that's all. Known each other since we were this tall." Kyle lowered his hand to his knee.

"She doesn't think so."

"What can I say?" He shrugged.

Liza rolled her eyes.

"Your lips are blue," he said.

"Duh. I told you the water was freezing," Liza said.

"So why'd you make us go swimming?"

Liza shook her head.

They sat on the cool sand and huddled together. Liza said, "Your family seems nice. You and your dad are funny."

"He thinks he's a lot funnier than he really is, but, you know, I go along. Don't want to hurt his feelings."

"How kind," Liza said.

"Are you being sarcastic?" Kyle put on a serious face.

"Me? Never."

Kyle scooted closer to Liza. She could feel his warmth. What was happening?

He placed a white ribbed shell in his hand. Liza examined it and said, "I used to collect shells all the time when we'd drive out to the beach. My mom finally told me to stop bringing them home because they were all over the place." She took it from his hand and tossed it into a small wave.

"When I was a kid, we'd try to find those big shells that you can hear the waves in. And sand crabs. Me and my brothers used to dig up a whole bunch and drop them on my sister while she was tanning."

"How mean." Liza made a face.

"We thought it was funny, but she didn't like it too much. I think she's forgiven us since then."

Liza snatched a stick and drew a heart in the wet sand. "I used to always put in the name of the boy I liked at school."

"Will this one have my name in it?" Kyle said with a smirk.

Liza felt her heart drop into her stomach and her face flush. Should she laugh it off or give in to her first temptation and slap him? She chose to laugh.

"Tell me more about your family," he said in a genuine tone.

Liza sat for a minute. She didn't want to go there. She wanted to enjoy the lingering colors of the sunset and, for a moment, think of nothing else but sitting on the beach, listening to the waves lap against the shore, and being with Kyle.

* * *

"Thanks for inviting me. I'm not sure I enjoyed the swim against my will, but all in all it was fun," Liza said. He opened her car door.

"How about church tomorrow?"

"Uh . . ."

"Come on, I'll save you a seat." Kyle grinned.

"I'll think about it. My mom and dad are gone and I better get home. Maybe next week or something?" Liza sat in the driver's seat and started the engine. He shut her door.

She chose the long way home so she could sort through her thoughts. Hopefully, her parents were talking and her family life would change back to the way it used to be, the way it was supposed to be. Her dad would put their family first and spend time with them this summer, especially now that she'd be busy in the fall attending college. And that decision still loomed over her. Should she accept the offer from Mr. Marcus and play for Oak? Or should she wait to see what other offers might come in? And what about this church thing? Kyle? Did he like her, or was he only trying to get her to be a Mormon? Could she be a Mormon? Would her mom want to go to church? What would her dad say? How were things at the Stratmore?

Her head ached. Too many questions and not enough answers. Maybe when she got home, she'd find something out about the most important thing, her parents.

Chapter Twenty-Three

The light flashed on the answering machine. Liza sat down and played the message. "Hi, it's Mom. Everything's going well. I hope you're doing okay. We'll see you in the morning."

Liza played the message again. Her mom's voice seemed filled with a long absent but familiar happiness. Liza repeated the words in her mind. *Everything's going well.* She breathed a sigh of relief.

Liza rushed up the stairs to her parents' bedroom—the only room with surround sound. She stepped over to the oak armoire and flipped on the television before flopping onto the neatly made bed. She surfed through a few channels and settled on something with Sandra Bullock. She'd choose another movie to follow that one.

She pulled the covers back and settled into her parents' bed for a long night of watching movies. Now that she knew things between her parents were going well, she anticipated relaxing and watching chick flicks.

She rummaged around the nightstand for the second remote, the one that turned on the surround sound. Not finding it there, she figured it must have fallen off. But she didn't see it on the floor either. She moved to her hands and knees to check under the bed.

Instead of the remote, she found a copy of the Book of Mormon. She picked it up and began thumbing through the pages, still sitting on the floor.

Her attention was drawn back to the movie, but after a few minutes, she once again returned to the Book of Mormon. She felt compelled to investigate what her mother had been reading and, she had to admit, she was curious about a book she assumed interested Kyle.

She began with the title page. She was surprised to find herself captivated almost immediately by the testimonies of those who'd seen the gold plates. She rose and sat on the edge of the bed as she began to read about Nephi. She continued to read the unfamiliar words and strange names. The language was more formal than she was used to. But it wasn't the words that persuaded her to keep reading; it was how she felt as she read.

She walked to the armoire and turned off the TV. Returning to the bed, she snuggled down into the covers. Page after page, chapter after chapter, she immersed herself in the stories of this strange book. The images washed over her as she learned of ancient people and their dealings with God. A comforting, safe feeling encompassed her.

She read late into the night until she could no longer keep her eyes open.

*   *   *

Liza awoke earlier than normal for a Sunday morning, especially after staying up so late reading. She stretched her arms and then stared at the ceiling, contemplating what she'd read. Was God real? Did He really care about people—about her? She'd never thought much about God. She'd lived her life from one day to the next, without much consideration of a supreme being. This morning, though, she found herself wondering about things she'd never thought about before.

She rose from the bed and noticed the soft morning light showering the trees in the front yard. She sashayed over to the master bathroom, peered at herself in the mirror, and finger styled her bangs. She pulled on her mom's printed silk robe and tied the belt around her trim waist. She picked up the Book of Mormon. It was almost nine-thirty. When would her parents come home?

Usually on Sunday mornings, everyone slept in and ate breakfast in shifts. When she was younger, though, the whole family used to get up and enjoy a big breakfast of eggs, bacon, pancakes, and fresh fruit. Since her dad started working so much, he frequently worked on Sundays, so their Sunday morning family breakfast subsided, like the rest of their traditions. This morning, though, she would not let any negative thoughts about her dad seep into her mind. Her whole body was crossed in hopes that her parents' weekend would put their family back on track. All of her wishing and hoping seemed like it might finally pay off.

Liza sat at the kitchen table and laid her head on it. She closed her eyes and recalled memories of breakfasts in their other house, their *real* home. She laughed out loud as she remembered the time when Jason was goofing around and accidentally flipped a scrambled egg across the table, which hit her dad right on the nose. Her father laughed and then launched a piece of *his* eggs, turning breakfast into an all-out food fight until her mom broke in, demanding the three of them clean the mess immediately. Her mom had stood there menacingly, a rag in her outstretched hand, until her dad flipped a small piece of egg that landed in her hair. She then joined in the food fight. Liza remembered how her mom landed in her dad's lap and they both laughed at each other. What great times they'd had.

Now it seemed more likely than ever that they'd have those happy family times again. Liza grinned.

"What's going on?" Jason asked. He lunged for the refrigerator. He grabbed a box of crackers off the top of the refrigerator.

"Just remembering the Sunday breakfasts we used to have." Liza sat back against the chair. She placed the Book of Mormon in her lap, under the table.

"Food fight." Jason nodded.

They both laughed. True, Jason annoyed her at times, but he was her little brother and she loved him, though she'd never admit that to him or anyone else.

"Did you enter your drawing in that contest at the Arts Center?" Liza looked at Jason.

"Yeah, but there was some pretty awesome stuff." Jason threw a small cracker up in the air and attempted to catch it in his mouth, but it dropped to the floor.

"I think your drawings are . . . okay, for a lame brother like you. That one of the volleyball player about to spike the ball is pretty good. I mean, it's okay." Liza mimicked a player throwing a ball in the air ready to spike it.

"They're going to announce the winners next weekend. First place is fifty bucks." Jason poured a glass of orange juice and drank it in one gulp.

"You're lucky."

"Yeah. I know." Jason leaned back in his chair.

"Seriously. You have volleyball *and* art. I only have basketball. I don't know what I'd do without basketball, I'd be completely lost. I guess if I accept the offer to play for Oak and even get a scholarship, I won't have to worry about finding anything else."

Jason burped.

"You're so disgusting," Liza said, crinkling her nose.

"And proud of it." Jason smiled.

Liza shook her head. "And, by the way, thanks for ditching me last night."

"Oooo," Jason said. "Liza's in love—"

"You're so—"

"Smart?" Jason raised and lowered his eyebrows a few times.

"No, that's not what I was thinking."

"Admit it."

"I can't. You're not smart. Sorry."

"Funny." Jason got up, pulled a bowl from the cupboard, and poured in cold cereal.

"Actually, Kyle is going on a mission or something for church."

"A what?" He poured milk in his bowl. It overflowed.

"A mission. At least that's what I've heard. I don't know exactly what it is, but he's not looking for a girlfriend. And if he was, I know one that'd love to fill in."

"You?"

"No. Jessica whatever her name is. Anyway, it doesn't matter."

Jason stuffed his mouth with too much cereal.

Liza retrieved the Book of Mormon from her lap and started reading.

"What's that?" Jason asked, drooling milk on the table.

"Nothing."

"Really, what book is it?"

"You mean, you know what a book is?"

Jason gave a hardy, obnoxious laugh. He yanked the book from Liza's hands. "Book of Mormon?"

Liza grabbed the book back. "If you have to know, it's like the Bible. It's Mom's book."

"What're you doing with it?"

"I found it last night and started reading it."

"Why would you read something you don't have to?"

Liza rolled her eyes. "It's Mom's and I wanted to see what she's been reading."

"So what's it about?" Jason shoveled more cereal into his mouth.

"Ancient people in America."

"Like Columbus?"

Liza slapped her forehead. "No. Before that. Before Jesus was even born."

Jason stared at her with a vacant look.

"You know, the reason why we have Christmas is because Jesus was born."

"Duh. I know that."

"Okay, well, I read it for a long time."

"Why?"

"Because, I felt, I don't know. Peaceful, I guess."

"Are you turning Mormon?"

"No . . . I don't know. I started reading because I was curious, but once I started . . . it's hard to explain."

"You're freaking me out, Liza."

"Forget it."

"Dad doesn't believe any of this religious stuff. He won't like it that you're reading a Bible book." Jason leaned back in his chair

"I think Mom's going to talk to him about it. She wants to go back to church." Liza played with the pages. "It's all pretty weird, I know, but there's something to this book. I can't explain it." She caressed the book.

"Don't Mormons have lots of wives and they all have to move to Utah or something?"

Liza stared at her brother. "That is the most ridiculous thing I've heard. Kyle's dad doesn't have a bunch of wives and they obviously don't live in Utah."

"But being a Mormon is like being in a cult."

"I've heard a few stories too, but Kyle seems normal, and it was actually fun last night. They had a bunch of people and great food. Kyle and his dad seem to be close. I wish Dad and I . . ." She didn't finish her sentence.

"You *are* turning Mormon."

"Don't be so lame. I think I might like to know more, that's all."

Jason shook his head. He moved to the couch in the family room. He stretched out and used the remote to turn on the television. He surfed channels, something that always bugged Liza because he scanned through channels so fast she couldn't even tell what was on the TV.

"I'm trying to read. Can't you do something else?"

"Nope."

"Fine. I'll leave then." Liza rose and gazed out the window. "Uh oh. Mom and Dad are pulling into the driveway. Mom won't like this mess."

Jason shrugged.

Liza shot him a look. "You're so lazy." She threw the pillows back on the couch and tossed Jason's shoes at him. She arranged the magazines on the table, grabbed some soda cans, and used her best aim to sink them into the trash can on the other side of the counter. She removed the candy wrappers from the table and threw them away and then placed the dirty dishes in the sink. She ran up the stairs and shoved the Book of Mormon back under the bed. She hurried back in time to meet her parents at the door.

"Hi, Mom. Dad," Liza said, trying not to breathe too heavy.

"What's going on?" Her mom glanced around the room as she entered with Liza's dad close behind.

"Nothing." Liza smiled, desperately wanting to know how things had gone. What had her mother said? How had her father reacted? What would their future hold?

"Everything here okay?" her mom asked.

"Yep. How was your weekend?" Liza asked with her fingers crossed behind her back.

Her parents said nothing but sat on the couch together, holding hands.

Her mom said, "We need to spend some time together as a family. We thought, maybe, we could go to the cabin next weekend."

Liza grinned as she watched her parents display more affection for each other than they'd shown in all the time put together since moving to Aldrich Heights. Things must have gone well at the hotel.

Chapter Twenty-Four

Liza woke seconds before her radio alarm started playing one of her favorite songs, definitely a positive sign. She lay in bed for a few minutes listening to the music and tossing her thoughts around.

She recalled playing in the ocean with Kyle and how much fun they'd had together. She'd felt a connection with him, and she was confident he'd felt the same. She laughed as she remembered Jessica's reaction when she caught them in the water, splashing each other. Today, she looked forward to seeing Kyle and embarking on a new phase of their relationship.

She laced her fingers and placed her hands behind her head as she replayed the previous day in her mind. It felt like old times, spending some of the day together as a family. Until, of course, the phone rang. Reality check. Her dad always leaped like a trained poodle when they called. He apologized, but it was the same disappearing act. Again. Did he mean what he said about the cabin? Would they go together or would work get in the way? She wanted to believe him. She needed to believe him.

She decided to concentrate on the happier events of the day

and refused to let fearful or angry thoughts ruin her hopes. After all, her parents had acted like couples at school. Mushy. Embarrassing. Wonderful. Something had changed, and she was certain it would lead to reuniting her whole family.

She fantasized about the trip to the cabin. Her mother's father left the cabin to them when he died almost ten years ago. At first, they visited it often and spent time fishing and hiking around the area. In the wintertime, they traveled to the cabin and played in the traces of snow that sometimes fell. She giggled when she remembered the time an unexpected storm doused the mountains with enough snow to make snowballs. She and Jason tried to attack her dad with a bunch of snowballs they'd stored for the right opportunity. He let them hit him a few times before he tackled them and buried them both in the new fallen powder. She remembered how the soft, cold snow made her tongue tingle.

Yes, the cabin equaled fun, happy memories. This trip would bring their family back together, she was sure of it. Things would be different. Actually, things would be the way they were supposed to be. Her goal was in sight, and she was determined to let nothing get in the way.

By the end of next weekend, her family would be back to normal, and the last year or so would only be a bad dream. This trip would bridge the gap between past and present and would pave the way for new memories. She was absolutely convinced of it.

"Liza?" came her mother's voice from the hall.

"Yes?"

"It's time for breakfast. You better hurry."

Liza glanced at the clock. More time than she realized had elapsed since she first awoke. She catapulted herself out of bed and hurried to her closet. She pulled on a pair of jeans and a plain yellow t-shirt.

She bounded down the hall toward the kitchen, expecting to see everyone seated around the breakfast table. She stopped in her tracks when she realized that she would be eating alone. She let out a sigh and walked to the pantry. She plopped down at the table and picked at a blueberry muffin. Her mom entered from the other direction.

"Where is everyone?" Liza asked.

"Jason had to be at school early, so I dropped him off a little while ago."

"Where's Dad?"

Her mom looked away. "How about some juice?"

"Mom? Where's Dad?"

Her mother cleared her throat. "He had to go in early and take care of some paperwork for his case this week."

Liza blinked her eyes several times.

"Now, Liza, please don't be upset. Your dad's trying to make amends, and I believe him when he says he wants to change his priorities. We all need to give him a little time to get things done at the office and it'll be different. He's going to work as much as he can this week so we'll be able to go to the cabin on Friday." She handed Liza a glass of grape juice. "We're all planning on it. You'll see."

Liza remained silent.

"I think this trip will start to set things right. It's a move in the right direction."

"I don't want anything to happen to our family. I want it to be like it used to be," Liza said.

"I know. Your dad has finally realized what his schedule has done to the family. Give him a little more time, and I think he'll come through for you, for all of us."

Liza hugged her mother. She smelled the soft scent of her perfume and felt the warmth of her skin.

"Now go on and get to school," her mom said.

Liza gulped the last of her juice, grabbed her backpack, and headed out the door.

*   *   *

"How was your weekend? Rumor has it you were with Kyle." Sara flung her newly dyed red hair behind her shoulders. They stood in front of Aldrich Heights High.

Liza stared at her. "Nice hair."

"Thanks, I did it myself." Sara moved her head from side to side.

"No one would ever know." Liza rolled her eyes.

"Tell me about your weekend with Kyle."

"How did you hear about it?"

"I saw Jason earlier. He sure is hot. Anyway, he mentioned something." Sara played with her hair.

"Jason's asking for it, when I see him—"

"Come on, tell."

"I went to a luau dinner and he was there. End of story." Liza shrugged.

"A luau, huh? Did he wear a grass skirt? Were you drooling the whole time, or what?"

"Sara, is your mind always in the same place?"

"Yeah, pretty much. Is there anything else besides guys?" Sara picked something out of her braces.

Liza shook her head. She was excited to see Kyle. They'd had fun at the luau, and he'd made it clear he wanted to spend time with her instead of with Jessica.

"Are you and Kyle gonna go out?" Sara asked.

Liza didn't say anything, but she smiled as she again recalled playing in the ocean and how it felt to be encased by Kyle's arms. She smiled wider as she remembered sitting on the soft, cool sand watching the sun dip below the distant horizon.

"I'd call that a big yes," Sara said, interrupting Liza's memories.

"Huh?"

"Don't look now, but there's Kyle coming up the ramp."

"He is?" Liza fingered her hair and ran her tongue over her teeth to clear out any embarrassing remains of breakfast. She drew in a deep breath.

Before Liza could turn around to face Kyle, Sara said, "Uh oh."

"What?"

"He's got his arm around Jessica."

"Excuse me?" Liza's stomach churned.

"Kyle and Jessica are over there." Sara motioned with her eyes.

Liza clenched her fists and bit her lip. She didn't turn around. Who did he think he was, playing her like that at the luau? He'd lied about his relationship with Jessica and made a fool out of Liza. She was less than amused.

She started walking briskly toward her first class. Sara followed right behind her.

"Liza?"

"I don't want to be late for class," Liza said over her shoulder. "I'll see you later." Liza picked up her speed and ran to the building. How could she have been so gullible?

Chapter Twenty-Five

Liza lounged on the leather couch in the living room.

Why did she feel like this? Her parents' trip to the Stratmore Hotel turned out even better than she'd hoped. It seemed that her family problems were working out and the trip to the cabin lay ahead. Her dad was still heavily involved in work, but he promised he'd make changes. Isn't that what he said? Of course, he'd broken so many promises that he didn't deserve her trust, yet she desperately wanted to believe that he'd change and they'd all be happy again. Her parents both said things would get better. She had to believe them.

The doorbell rang.

So why did she feel like someone just kicked her in the stomach? Simple. Kyle. She'd had a crush on him for so long, and when he'd paid so much attention to her at the luau, she'd thought maybe they'd get together. But today, knowing he was with Jessica riled her anger and confused her at the same time. He said he and Jessica were just friends. Were they?

Didn't matter. She planned to avoid Kyle for the rest of her life. He'd never play her again, that's for sure.

She heard the doorbell again. She didn't want to answer it, so she lay there like a slug.

"Liza? Can you please get that?" Her mom's voice echoed from upstairs.

Liza sighed and rose from the couch. She shuffled to the door, wishing that whoever stood on the other side would get tired of waiting and leave, but the bell continued to ring.

She opened the door. "Mr. Reynolds?" The blood rushed from her face as she searched for Kyle. He was the last person she wanted to see.

"Hi, Liza. Is your mom home?" He stood there in a blue dress shirt and dark dress pants. His blond hair was thinner than Kyle's but still covered his head. Thankfully, he'd come alone.

"Yes, would you like to come in?" She left him waiting in the entry hall.

Liza took the stairs three at a time. She entered her mom's room. "Mr. Reynolds, Kyle's dad, is downstairs. He wants to talk to you."

Liza and her mom descended the stairs. "Hello," her mom said.

"How are you today?" Mr. Reynolds smiled and extended his hand.

Liza's mom shook his hand. "We're fine, thanks."

"I'm David Reynolds. I met Liza at the luau Saturday evening. I called the other night and left a message."

"Yes. I'm sorry I didn't return your call." She glanced at Liza. "Would you like to sit down?" Her mom motioned to the couch in the living room.

Mr. Reynolds held his hand up. "Thank you, I don't want to impose. My son Kyle mentioned that you are a member of the Church."

"Yes, I was baptized many, many years ago. I haven't been for some time, but I think I'm interested in attending again."

"I live a few streets over. I'm a member of the bishopric. Would you mind if I came by for a visit this week?"

"I'd like that. I've spoken to my husband about going back

to church. He's still not interested in any kind of religion, but he said he wouldn't mind if the kids and I talked to you." Liza noticed a new light in her mom's eyes.

"When would be a good time?"

"I think Wednesday evening would work," Liza's mom said.

"We can be here about seven. I'll bring some of my wife's apple pie." Mr. Reynolds's smile communicated a genuine concern for them.

"Thank you. We'll see you Wednesday night." Her mom sounded happy.

Mr. Reynolds shook their hands and left. Liza shut the door and leaned against it. What if he brought Kyle? What would she do? Her heart beat faster and faster. She'd have to avoid the visit; it was the only solution. She'd find somewhere else to be on Wednesday night.

"Liza," her mother said.

"Yeah?"

"Will you stay for his visit?"

Liza shrugged.

"Would you consider reading some of the Book of Mormon before his visit?" Her mom's gaze was fixed on her. Liza turned and walked toward the kitchen. Her mother followed.

Liza sat at the table and tapped her fingers on the tabletop. "I have a confession."

"You do?"

"While you were at the hotel, I decided to sleep in your bed so I could watch some movies."

"I know," her mom said. "You never made the bed."

"That's not the confession."

Her mom furrowed her brows. "What is?"

"I found your Book of Mormon under the bed."

"You did?"

"I stayed up late reading some of it."

"What did you think?" Her mom's eyes widened.

"It was a little strange. Some of the names were weird, but I felt . . . warm inside. I've never felt that way before."

"That's how I feel when I read it too. It's a wonderful, peaceful, happy feeling."

"Yeah."

"And?"

"I don't know. Maybe I'd like to know more."

"Really? You would?" Her mother's face seemed to shine.

Liza nodded.

"Then you'll be here on Wednesday night?"

Liza couldn't deny what she felt when she read from the Book of Mormon and she could hardly disappoint her mom, but she did not want to be around Kyle.

"You may find what I did when I was about your age." Her mom reached over and gave Liza's arm a squeeze.

"As long as I don't have to sit by Kyle," Liza muttered to herself.

Chapter Twenty-Six

Tuesday, after school, Liza entered Oak University's brown brick gymnasium. As she stood in the entryway, memories of the championship game flooded her mind. A smile crossed her lips as she relived her last free throw and the exhilaration she felt on that magical night when the basketball fell through the hoop and landed her team in Aldrich Heights High School history.

She heard the women's team playing in the gym. She stepped over to the drinking fountain and gulped some cold water to moisten her dry throat. Finally, she pushed open the large gym doors.

The lights were on, but the bleachers weren't extended. She spied the team at the other end of the gym running through some drills. She noticed two men. One of them caught a glimpse of her and immediately headed in her direction.

"Hello, can I help you?" he asked in a friendly tone. He stood head to head with Liza. He was of average weight and had light brown hair that was parted in the middle.

"My name is Liza Compton and Mr. Marcus said it would be okay to stop by and catch a practice." Liza shuffled her feet.

"Yes, I know who you are. Mr. Marcus mentioned his visit with you. I'm Coach Blacke." He shook her hand.

Coach Blacke blew his whistle. The women turned toward him. He cupped his hands around his mouth and said in a loud voice, "Everyone, take a break and come on over here." He motioned with his arm.

"This is Liza Compton. She's come by to watch our practice," Coach Blacke said. He introduced each of the young women on the team, who, in turn, spoke to Liza.

"Back to practice, ladies," Coach Blacke said.

Liza watched them race back to the court and fall into a practice drill led by Mr. King, a tall, thin man, who was the assistant coach.

The team consisted of several young women. One, with short blonde hair, stood over six feet tall and obviously played the center position. A few others were about Liza's height and probably played the forward position, as she would if she joined the team. The guards were all shorter, but she could see their quick responses and ball-handling skills. Liza noticed the captain, who called out to the players. As Liza scrutinized their drills, excitement washed over her like a wave of cool, invigorating sea water.

"I'm glad you stopped by, Liza. I watched your game the other night and you played well. I'd like you to play for me. I think you have excellent shooting strength, and you defend well too," Coach Blacke said.

"Thanks. I love basketball. My mom says I eat, drink, and breathe it." She beamed.

"It shows. You'd be a great addition to the team."

"Thank you."

"I better get back to practice, but feel free to look at the locker room and the display cases along the hall. The Lady Hawks have been conference champions the last two years running. We also won the tournament championship against Northgate University the year before last. I think you'd enjoy the program."

Coach Blacke ran back to the team. He appeared to be in good shape and about the age of her dad.

Liza strolled through the locker room and down the hall. She gazed at the award case for a while and admired the many awards that adorned the shelves. She laughed out loud at a photo of what must've been the original team. Times had changed. Uniforms and hairstyles had changed. Coaches had changed.

Liza stared at her reflection in the glass. Basketball. Whatever else in her life confused her, one thing didn't. Basketball. She knew basketball. On the court she was in charge. It was the constant in her life. If she didn't have basketball . . . she couldn't even consider that.

Chapter Twenty-Seven

"Come in." Liza's mom opened the door wide, and Liza watched Kyle and his dad walk through the entryway and into the living room. They both wore dress pants, white dress shirts, and ties. Though she'd never seen him dressed so formally, Kyle looked better than she'd ever seen him. She bit her lip because, as she reminded herself, he was a player and he wasn't at all interested in her. Did he think she hadn't observed his attachment to Jessica since the luau? She was proud that she'd successfully avoided him for the last few days, though she was sure he hadn't noticed.

"Hey, Liza. How's it going? I haven't seen you around school." Kyle grinned with his perfect teeth.

"I've been, um, busy." She feigned a smile. Maybe he had noticed, but it didn't change the fact that he'd lied about his relationship with Jessica and she had no plans to keep him entertained during Jessica's absence.

Liza's mom pointed to the couch. "Go ahead and sit down. Jason should be home any minute. My husband won't be joining us. He's working late tonight."

"Here's the apple pie I promised," Kyle's dad said. He handed the pie to Liza.

"I've got the ice cream. I'll take it into the kitchen with you," Kyle said. He followed Liza into the kitchen.

Liza placed the pie on the island and placed the ice cream in the freezer.

Kyle smiled. "What've you been busy with?"

"School stuff."

Kyle cocked his head to the side. "Something wrong?"

"Nope."

"You seem mad."

"Do I?"

Kyle nodded.

"How'd you manage to pull yourself away from Jessica tonight?" She said it with much more emotion than she'd intended.

"Huh?"

Liza gave him a look.

Kyle grabbed her arm. Despite her best effort to be unaffected by him, his touch made her stomach flip-flop. "What are you talking about?"

"I've seen you two at school."

"We're friends, that's all. I told you that at the luau."

Liza raised her eyebrow. "Friends with benefits."

"Benefits?"

"You know, arms around each other. Stuff like that."

Kyle grinned.

"What?"

"If I didn't know better I'd think you were—"

"We better get back to the other room. I told my mom I'd listen to you." Liza wiped her moist hands on her pants and left the kitchen before Kyle could say anything else.

The front door flung open, and Jason staggered into the entryway. "Sorry I'm late, Mom. Colin's car stalled at the beach."

"Come in and sit down," Liza's mom said.

Liza glanced at Jason, who wore a dopey expression. He gave

her a cheesy grin, and she could instantly read his thoughts.

"Thanks for letting us come by. Kyle and I like to visit families, and we're both happy to be here. Can we start with a word of prayer?"

"That would be lovely," Liza's mom said.

Kyle and his dad bowed their heads. Liza followed suit. Kyle offered a simple yet beautiful prayer. Liza softened after hearing him pray, and she found she wasn't as upset about seeing him with Jessica. She didn't understand it, but she felt something she couldn't explain. It was similar to what she felt when she read from the Book of Mormon.

"Sister Compton, you were baptized many years ago, is that right?" Mr. Reynolds asked.

Sister? A strange way to address someone that wasn't a nun.

"Yes, in college. But I haven't been involved with the Church for twenty years or more. And I haven't ever shared it with my kids." Her mom gave a weak smile.

"What if we start from the beginning?" Mr. Reynolds suggested in a comforting way.

Her mom nodded. "That'd be perfect."

Kyle's dad continued, "I'd like to share what we call the plan of salvation or plan of happiness with you and your family tonight. I've asked Kyle to start us off."

Kyle moved to the edge of his seat. "A long time ago, before we were actually born, we lived with Heavenly Father. We lived together as brothers and sisters. We knew each other and we loved each other. Then, one day, we were presented a plan about coming here to earth."

Kyle's eyes sparkled while he calmly explained the most outrageous story Liza had ever heard. Strange as it was, though, a certain sense of peace settled on her as Kyle continued to explain the plan of salvation. She found herself drawn into the fantastic tale.

After several minutes, Kyle stopped and turned to his father.

"If we follow the gospel of Jesus Christ, we can live with Heavenly Father again and we can also be with our families. We believe that death does not end family relationships, but that we can still enjoy our families even after death. Birth, mortality, and death are all steps in our eternal life." Mr. Reynolds stopped for a moment. "Any questions?"

Liza and Jason both shook their heads. Liza's mother said, "Please, go on."

Mr. Reynolds continued, "Heavenly Father has also blessed us to know that there's a plan. Nothing happens that He doesn't know. We each have a plan for our own individual lives."

Jason raised his hand.

"Yes?" Mr. Reynolds asked.

"I've heard Mormons worship some Joseph Smith guy," Jason said.

"Jason." Liza's mom frowned at him.

"We believe that Joseph Smith restored the gospel to us, but we worship God, not Joseph Smith," Mr. Reynolds said.

Mr. Reynolds glanced around the room. "Any other questions?"

Liza and Jason exchanged glances. Liza could still feel something with which she wasn't familiar. It was warm, reassuring, but odd.

"Thank you for letting us share this with you tonight. I believe the Holy Ghost has witnessed the truth of our message here tonight," Mr. Reynolds said.

"It's been a long time since I've felt that. I've missed it," Liza's mom said. She wiped at her eyes.

"Thank you, Sister Compton. We'd like to invite you to attend church. We meet in the building on Magnolia Street at nine in the morning," Mr. Reynolds said.

"I think I know where that is. I've driven past it a few times. White brick?"

"Yes, that's it. We'd love to see you there on Sunday," Mr. Reynolds said.

"We're planning a trip to our family cabin this weekend, but I'd like to make it back to attend church. It's been such a long time."

Mr. Reynolds smiled. He said, "I think you'll find our ward friendly and welcoming."

"Thank you."

"May we have a prayer?" Mr. Reynolds asked.

Liza's mom nodded her head.

"Would you offer it, Sister Compton?"

"It's been so long since I've prayed in front of people."

"Say what's in your heart." Mr. Reynolds's face conveyed a certain confidence.

Liza's mom offered the prayer. Liza listened to a combination of words she'd never heard her mother use. She'd never felt this close to her mom.

When the prayer ended, Liza studied her mom. Her mother's eyes glistened, and Liza wanted to rush over and embrace her. She wasn't sure what had happened tonight.

Her mom said, "Liza, can you go slice the pie?"

"Sure."

"I'll help," Kyle said. He jumped to his feet and followed Liza. "I think we need to finish our conversation."

"About what?" Liza turned around and grabbed some plates from the cupboard.

He stepped so close behind her that she felt his breath on the back of her neck. Goose bumps erupted on her arms while she struggled to keep the plates from dropping to the ground. Finally, she stepped to the side and turned to face him.

"Jessica," he said.

Liza blinked her eyes. "Who?"

Kyle moved in close, face to face, with only the pile of plates separating them. "Jess and I are friends. Nothing more." He held up his right hand and said, "Scout's honor."

Their gaze locked. Liza's heart pounded in her ears.

"Where's my pie?" Jason said as he bounded into the room.

Liza cleared her throat. She stepped to the island and clumsily put the plates down. She sliced the pie, placed a piece on one of the plates, and handed it to Jason.

"What about my ice cream?"

"Huh?"

Jason looked from Liza to Kyle and back to Liza. "Did I interrupt something?" he asked with a smirk.

Liza shook her head. "No." She plopped some ice cream on top of his pie.

After they'd dished up the dessert for everyone, Kyle grabbed his plate of pie and ice cream and motioned for Liza to follow him to the patio. They sat at a glass table with matching patio chairs and Kyle said, "Are we clear about Jessica?"

"Yeah." Liza gave him a sideways glance.

After a few moments of silence, Kyle said, "What'd you think about what my dad and I said?"

"I'm not sure."

Kyle took a bite of pie. As if reading Liza's thoughts, he said, "Did you feel something?"

In a soft voice Liza said, "Yeah, I did. I don't know how to explain it."

"It was the Holy Ghost telling you that what we were teaching was true."

"Oh."

Liza used her spoon to play with the ice cream. "This is kind of strange. I mean, I don't want to be rude, but I've never thought about these kinds of things. We've never had church stuff at home. I only found out that my mom was Mormon a few days ago."

"How come you didn't know?" Kyle finished off his pie.

"She said it's because her parents were so mad and my dad didn't want any religion."

"Seems like she wants to get involved again."

"Yeah, it does, but—"

"What?" He peered at her.

"You wouldn't understand."

"Try me."

Liza studied Kyle. True, his shiny blond hair, sky blue eyes, and perfect smile left her breathless, but there was more to him. Something deeper. Perhaps she'd misjudged his relationship with Jessica. She'd been guilty of rash judgments before. Maybe he wasn't a player after all.

She couldn't translate her thoughts into words. She didn't understand what was happening. She never thought she'd ever be sitting in her backyard talking to Kyle Reynolds, especially about religion.

"My dad . . ."

"Are you worried he'll have a bad reaction?"

"My mom said he wasn't happy about this when they were first together. You and your dad, you're lucky."

"How's that?"

"You get along so well and you have fun. I wish . . . I don't want to make my dad upset or anything. I know my mom said he was okay with this, but I'm not sure."

"Are there problems with your dad?"

Liza argued with herself as to whether or not she should say any more about her father. She didn't want to scare Kyle away; yet, he had a way of replacing her fears with trust.

"He's been really busy. He's not home much, and when he is, it's not much fun. He's been so involved with some big case that he missed my championship game. He even missed a meeting over at Oak."

"Oak?"

Liza glanced at the ground. "I've been offered a spot on the team and possibly even a scholarship."

"That's so cool. Way to go." Kyle reached over and laid a congratulating hand on her shoulder.

"Thanks." Liza's smile covered her entire face.

Kyle gazed at Liza and her heart skipped a beat. "I'm glad we came over tonight."

"Me too."

Mr. Reynolds poked his head out the door. "Kyle, we need to head home."

"Okay, Dad." Kyle turned to Liza. "See you tomorrow?" His smile infected her.

Liza nodded.

She watched Kyle walk into the house. She sat back in her chair and gazed up at the sky. Her mind spun in all sorts of directions. She tried to make sense of it all.

Thoughts of her dad surfaced. He'd made promises to change, but she didn't see any evidence to back up his claims.

Would they really make it to the cabin?

She was still excited about her offer to play with Oak, but she hadn't yet made a final decision.

Now Kyle.

And the Church.

"Liza? Can I come out?" her mom asked.

"Sure, Mom."

Liza's mom sat in the chair closest to Liza. "Any thoughts about tonight?"

"Truthfully?"

"Yes."

"I have so many things going on in my head I don't even know where to start. I don't know what to think." She blinked her eyes a few times.

"I believe everything they said. I've believed it for years only—"

"What about Dad?"

"What do you mean?" Her mom leaned in closer.

"Will this bother him?"

"I don't think so. He said he was fine with it."

"Are you sure?"

"Liza, your dad and I both agreed that we needed to make some changes. This is something I need to do. I hope, maybe, he'll be interested. Someday. I hope—"

"That Jason and I will want to be Mormons?"

"Yes."

"What if we don't?"

"You'll always be my daughter, and no matter what, I will always love you. I think, though, if you'll give this a chance you'll realize that it's true. I think it'll make our family stronger and better."

Stronger and better? A definite plus.

"As Kyle's dad spoke I remembered so many feelings I've buried. It felt wonderful to have those feelings again and be able to share them."

Liza noticed the light in her mother's eyes. Her mom appeared years younger and seemed elated. Maybe this was exactly what her family needed. Maybe this was the answer.

Chapter Twenty-Eight

Liza raced in the door. Friday, at last. The past few days had passed as slowly as the weeks just prior to summer break. Each day seemed to drag on and on and on. Basketball practice had been suspended, and she spent her class time doodling on her notebook and daydreaming of the cabin trip.

She had talked to Kyle a few times at school. Jessica was never far behind, though. Their conversation had been limited to the weather, Kyle's upcoming track meet, and how to get through the last stages of senioritis. Kyle mentioned bringing missionaries to her house when he and his dad returned for a visit.

She'd worked hard during the week to conceal her disappointment in her father's continued absence at home. He'd promised that the weekend would be something she wouldn't forget and she desperately wanted to believe him, though this would be his last chance to prove himself.

"Mom?" Liza yelled from the marble-tiled entryway.

"I'm in my room."

Liza ran up the stairs. She didn't want to waste a single

minute. She wanted to hit the road and head toward the cabin and their renewed life together as a family.

"Is Dad home yet?"

"No. Did you see Jason?" Her mom packed a sweatshirt and some pajamas in the familiar black suitcase.

"I'll go get my stuff ready. Now," Liza paused, "Dad will really be here, right? I mean, he's planning to come home and go with us, right?"

Her mother kept packing her suitcase.

"Mom, what's going on? You aren't answering me."

Her mom looked up and said, "Your dad called about an hour ago and said he needed to finish a few things. He was going to be in court but thought he'd be done in time for dinner. He asked us to meet him at the restaurant."

Liza stared at the floor and shook her head. She knew it; she knew he'd mess everything up. All those things he'd said, he didn't mean any of them.

"Go get ready, Liza."

Liza glanced at her mother. Even though she wanted to scream, she didn't want to cause her mom any grief.

"I'll bring my suitcase to the back door." She forced a smile.

"Liza?"

"Yeah?"

"He'll be there. I really think he's serious about changing."

"You do?"

"He was sincere last weekend. He's actually called me every day this week. He came home late last night. We stayed up talking and he listened to me. We had a real conversation for the first time in a long time."

"You think he'll keep his promise for the weekend?"

"I do. I truly believe he wants to make our family strong again. We may need to be patient, but I think he's trying."

"Okay," she said with as much enthusiasm as she could.

Her mom walked over and gently placed her arms around Liza. Liza rested her head on her mom's shoulder. She could smell the familiar fragrance in her mother's hair.

"Please, don't give up on him."

Liza pulled away from her mom. "Okay," Liza said with more conviction this time.

* * *

"Liza? Jason? Do you have all of your stuff? I'm ready to put it in the car."

Liza and Jason both hurried to the hallway with their bags.

"Did you pack your whole room or what?" Jason chided Liza.

"Did you even bring a change of underwear?" Liza shot back.

"That's enough. Both of you, take your things out to the car. Jason, please come back in and get this suitcase."

While they drove to the restaurant, Liza and Jason had a radio war, each wanting to listen to a different station and arguing over which music was the best. Finally, Liza's mom solved the problem and turned the radio off.

"Come on, you two, no arguing tonight. Please?"

Liza and Jason were both silent until Liza spoke. "Sorry, Mom."

"Yeah, sorry," Jason said.

"Here's the restaurant. It's pretty crowded. I guess we'll park over there. Do either of you see Dad's car?"

"No. I'm sure he'll be here soon, right?" Liza asked. She was trying her hardest to be positive and believe in her dad, even if it was becoming more and more difficult.

"He'll probably be a no-show, as usual," Jason said.

Liza's mom stopped the car in the nearest parking space and turned back to face Jason, who was sprawled across the back seat. "This is the rule for tonight: nothing bad about your father. No comments, no rolling of the eyes, nothing. He'll be here, and we are going to spend the weekend together like we've planned. Please, Jason, give him a chance."

"Yeah, well, he talked about all these changes, but it's been the same as always this whole week," Jason said.

"I know it's been difficult for both of you. Your dad wants

another chance. He wants to make things right. I don't think he realized how much he's been working and how that's made you both feel. I told him it wouldn't be easy to make these changes and that both of you are a little resentful of our move to Aldrich Heights. I also told him that it'd take some time, but it needed to start now." She reached out and took Jason's hand. "Nothing will change if we don't give him the chance. We all want the same thing, and tonight may be the beginning. We can't give up on our family."

"Fine," Jason said.

Liza and Jason exchanged glances. No need for words.

The three of them exited the blue BMW and walked toward the restaurant's entrance. A chubby hostess in a black dress greeted them and showed them to a table in the back. A busboy brought them each a glass of water and placed another glass on the table.

"Why don't we see what's on the menu? I can order something for Dad, and it'll be ready when he gets here." Liza's mom opened the menu.

Liza picked up the menu lying in front of her.

Jason grabbed his menu. "I think I'll have one of these big steaks." He puffed out his chest and said, "I have to keep looking good, you know. I wouldn't want to disappoint any of the beautiful women that admire me."

Liza and her mom burst out laughing.

"What?" Jason seemed bewildered.

"You're such a—" Liza started to say.

"I need to be lookin' good when you go to Oak so I can take all those college women out."

"Uh huh." Liza laughed again.

"Have you made a final decision about Oak?" Liza's mom asked. She sipped her water.

"Not yet. I was really impressed with Coach Blacke and the team."

Liza's mom took another sip of water. "Did you get the letter that came in the mail from Northern Cal?"

"Nope. I didn't see it."

"You'll have to read it after we get back and let us know what it says. It may be the first of many schools that are interested in you," her mother said.

"Maybe, but I think I really want to play for Oak." Liza sipped her water.

"Your dad and I would be thrilled to have you stay close to home and play for Oak."

"I guess you were pretty good at that championship game," Jason said.

Liza feigned shock. "All this time, I thought you were checking out the girls and didn't even realize I was on the team."

Jason patted Liza on the back. "I was watching you, maybe not the whole time, but I was watching."

"I think someone else was watching too," her mom said.

"Mom!"

"Oooo, Kyle," Jason said. He assumed a statuesque pose.

Liza glanced around the room and lowered her head.

"I noticed you were in a deep conversation when he and his dad were over. I think he likes you." Her mom smiled.

"Liza's got Kyle-fever," Jason said in a low voice.

Liza slapped Jason on the leg. Her face flushed. "I talked to him at school, and he asked me to find out if he and his dad could come over again next week."

"More church talk?" Jason asked.

Liza glared at him.

"You only want him to come over so you can stare at him," Jason said.

"For your information, I've been thinking about some of the things they said the other night."

"You have?" her mom asked.

Liza turned to her mom. "Some of the stuff sounded kind of weird, but I felt something calm and peaceful. I think we should have them come back."

"Of course you do," Jason said.

"Jason, really. I admit that Kyle's hot, but he and his dad said some things that I think might be true. That's all."

"I'm so happy you've thought about it. Tell him next week would be fine."

"He said they might bring some missionaries, if that's okay with you." Liza smoothed her hair.

"That'd be wonderful. What about you, Jason? Did you think about anything they said?"

He shrugged. "I think Liza wants Kyle to come over so she can stalk him."

"You're so mature," Liza said.

"Maybe he'll ask you to the prom," Jason said. He snatched a piece of bread from the basket in front of him.

Liza scowled at him.

Jason and Liza continued to argue back and forth when her mother's cell phone rang.

"Hello?" her mom answered. "I can't hear you very well. Hang on while I go outside the restaurant." She rose and left the dining room.

"What's that about?" Jason asked.

"Guess," Liza said.

"Dad?"

"I'm sure he's got some excuse for being late. I'm so sick of this," Liza said. She didn't need to hide her feelings from Jason.

"He's been a definite loser lately." Jason flipped a piece of ice across the table.

"I just hope—"

Liza glanced up to see her mother only a few feet from their table. Her mom sat down and said, "That was your dad."

"Really?" Liza tried to sound genuine.

"He said he's running late and we should go ahead and eat."

Liza broke in, "Oh, please, this is exactly what I expected."

"Calm down. He's still going to meet us at the cabin." Her mom gave her a look.

"Yeah right. He said he'd meet us for dinner and, well, I don't see him anywhere. He's great at the invisible father thing."

She tried to keep her words from spilling out, but they seemed to have a mind of their own.

"Liza, that's enough. Let's eat and then we'll drive to the cabin. He'll meet us there." Her mom's face showed no emotion.

Liza's voice cracked as she said, "Mom, you're not dealing with reality here. He's not coming. He's got something going at the office, again, and he won't make it. We'll waste a trip to the cabin. We might as well go home and save ourselves the trouble. Dad isn't going to change, and he won't meet us at the cabin." Her mouth rushed ahead of her brain, and she couldn't stop her words from oozing out and sticking to everyone around her.

"Liza, stop it. He's finishing up a big case and he has paperwork. He's doing the best he can."

"You still think he'll meet us at the cabin?"

"Yes. I told you earlier that I think he's sincere."

"But not long ago you were ready to ask him to leave."

Her mother gave a sigh. "You're right. I was. I thought that was the answer, but I was wrong. After our weekend at the hotel and this past week, he's shown me that he genuinely wants to make things better for all of us."

Liza rested her head on her hand. "Why does it have to be so hard?"

Her mom leaned over and placed her arm around Liza. "It'll work out, you'll see. It may not be exactly as you planned it, but it will work out."

Chapter Twenty-Nine

"Come on, Jason, hand me that little red bag," Liza said as she stood next to the trunk of the car.

"Where?"

"Duh, it's right in front of you." Liza stretched her arms and yawned. "Sure seems like it took longer than half an hour to get here."

Jason reached in and grabbed the bag. "Here. Oh, you're welcome."

"Thanks."

Liza hurried from the car to the porch of the rustic cabin, stopping to admire the clear sky and brilliant stars. She inhaled the crisp, clean air laced with a faint evergreen scent. Then she stepped inside, checked her watch, and started the countdown for her father's arrival. After all, if he was really serious about making changes and putting their family first, he wouldn't let them down, would he?

Jason was immediately behind her. "Where should I put these suitcases, Mom?" Jason dropped them to the floor.

"Right there will be fine, I guess. Thank you." Her mom turned on one of the lamps.

Jason removed the fireplace screen. With a poker he pushed some old, partially burned logs around.

"It's cold in here," Liza said. She rubbed her arms and then blew on her hands.

"Let's see if we can talk your brother into starting a fire. It'll be nice and cozy when Dad gets here. Jason, when you've brought in everything from the car, can you find some wood?"

"Sure, Mom." He saluted and then turned and left.

Liza sat on the small navy blue upholstered couch. "Did your family used to come up here very much?"

Her mom sat next to her. "We came up here quite a bit, actually. When I was a little girl, my dad would take us fishing and hiking. When we'd get back, Grandma would have stew or hamburgers waiting for us. I can almost smell it right now." She drew a deep breath through her nose. "I have so many happy memories of this place." She gazed around the room.

"I remember being here with you and Dad. It's been a long time, though." Liza laid her head on her mom's shoulder.

The door flung open. "It's so cool up here, exactly like I remember it. Let's live here." Jason stood in the doorway with a knitted cap on.

Liza giggled. "You're such a dork in that hat."

"At least my head's not freezing off my body."

"Speaking of not freezing," Liza's mom said as she tilted her head toward the fireplace.

He set some plastic bags filled with groceries on the oval wooden table. "I know, I know, go get some wood and build . . ." His sentence trailed off as he left the cabin.

* * *

After sipping hot chocolate and roasting a few marshmallows, Liza's mom stood and started pacing.

"We should go to bed. He's not coming," Liza said. She poured herself another cup of hot chocolate.

Her mom said nothing. She walked over to the refrigerator and opened the door. She surveyed the contents inside. "For lunch tomorrow we can have some salad and I'll make hamburgers. Would you guys like that? Jason, did you bring the sack in with the chips?"

"Yep." Jason flicked a piece of paper toward the fire.

"We're all set for a fun weekend. Maybe we can go out hiking tomorrow morning and see what wildlife we can spot. How does that sound? You two used to love searching for squirrels."

"Great, Mom." Jason tossed another paper on the fire.

Liza lay on the couch staring at the ceiling. "What should we do now?"

"I admit, it's been a while since we arrived." Her mom parted the white curtains on the kitchen window and peeked out.

Liza checked her watch. "Only two hours, that's all."

"I'll try him on his cell phone." Her mom reached into her purse and pulled out a flip phone. "I'll see if there's signal outside." She opened the front door and walked out.

"Dad is such a liar. All his big promises to spend the weekend with us. I actually believed he meant it. I don't know why I believed him, but I did," Liza said. She covered her face with the crook of her elbow.

"I say we go to sleep," Jason said as he yawned.

Her mom entered the cabin. "I called a few times, but only reached his voice mail. Maybe he's on the road and can't get a signal."

"Probably," Liza said without removing her arm from her face.

"Or maybe he had car trouble and can't get a signal," her mom said.

"Uh huh." Liza didn't believe for a second her dad's car was broken down on the side of the road or that he'd tried to call. He was obviously at work and was going to, once again, blow off the family for his job. What a waste of a weekend. And what a waste of hope that he meant what he'd said.

After several minutes, her mother stepped outside again. She returned and said, "I still can only reach his voice mail."

"I'm tired," Jason said.

"Me too," Liza said. She uncovered her face. "Let's go to bed." She wanted to lose herself in sleep so she could forget about her father's empty promises.

"I think we should drive back to the city and look for him. Maybe he has a flat tire and needs help."

"Drive back tonight? Now?" Jason exclaimed. He pulled a blanket over himself.

Liza chimed in, "We don't want to drive all the way back to the city tonight. I hate that road, especially at night."

"You're just scared of all the twists and turns and scary shadows," Jason said adding a few sound effects and waving his fingers.

"Am not."

"Are too."

"Am not."

"Are—"

Liza's mom cut in, "Let's go."

"Come on, Mom," Jason said.

"Dad's at work, we all know it. He promised—"

Her mother cut her off. "You're right, he did promise and I believe him. I think we should go back because there must be something wrong. Please, let's get in the car," her mother pleaded.

Liza gave a strong sigh and said, "Fine. I give up. Let's go. Dibs on front seat." Liza started toward the door.

"No way, it's my turn."

"Is not."

"Yes, it is."

"He's right, Liza," her mom said.

"Whatever," Liza said over her shoulder.

In the car Liza's mom said, "Put on your seat belts." She said it every time before she started the engine.

Liza put hers on and then leaned toward the door. She shook her head. This was the last straw. He'd proven it again; he didn't care about their family anymore. Her eyes burned.

Liza clenched her jaw. He wasn't her dad. He was someone she didn't know, and he'd disappointed her for the last time. This was it. No more chances.

She laid her head back and listened to the hum of the engine while they traveled along the road.

They'd waste a trip all the way back to the city and then what? Once her mom was convinced that her dad was going to blow off their family weekend, would they return to the cabin without him? Would they go home?

Her fury grew. She wanted to get home and forget about the whole weekend. It had been a huge mistake to believe that this weekend would be the turning point for her family. What a joke.

Liza's stomach flip-flopped as the road wound back and forth around the hills. The late hour left the unlit road deserted. The moonlight bathed the trees and illuminated sheer cliffs, giving Liza an eerie, uneasy feeling.

Finally, the narrow road straightened out a bit and she saw headlights in the distance, which made her feel a bit more at ease.

As the oncoming vehicle approached, Liza sat up in the back and squinted her eyes. "Is that car in our lane?"

"I don't think so." Her mom adjusted her glasses.

The other car closed in. Without warning, it swerved, clipping their car on the front end of the driver's side.

Liza felt the sudden impact and heard a rush of air as the air bags deployed. Metal scratched against metal. The tires screeched and the car moaned as they veered off the shoulder and became airborne.

Thud. Shatter. Thud. Glass shards rained inside the car. Liza could hear the car hit the boulders on the hillside.

Up, down, around. Up, down, around. Her stomach lurched back and forth while they somersaulted. The seat belt burned her skin as it dug into her neck.

She attempted to scream but nothing came out. Intense pain encompassed her right arm, like someone had jumped on it with cleats. Her face hit against the inside of the car. She couldn't tell which direction she faced. A warm substance cascaded down her head, and then . . . nothing.

Chapter Thirty

"She's awake. Call for the doctor," said the unfamiliar, distant voice.

Liza struggled to focus on her surroundings. She blinked several times and tried to raise her head. A strange woman dressed in green pants and a print jacket reached for Liza's left arm.

"Who are you? Where am I?" Liza eked out.

The woman patted her shoulder and said in a soft voice, "Don't worry, everything will be fine."

"What?" Liza couldn't understand her. The woman's words sounded garbled, like she was talking under water.

"The doctor will be in to see you soon." The woman pulled at Liza's pillow and stroked her head.

The woman walked away and stood in the doorway, where she spoke to another unfamiliar woman in a mumbled voice. After a few moments, both women left.

Liza's eyes focused more clearly. She was in a bed in a sterile-looking room. A window to her right showcased the setting sun. The curtains that surrounded the window were a beige, rose, and green design and matched a wallpaper border that lined the wall where it met the ceiling. The walls were painted an off-white. A shelf on the opposite wall held several vases filled with flowers.

She raised her left arm above her stomach and saw the IV attached to it. Then she examined her right arm and discovered that it was wrapped with a bandage and secured to her chest. She used her free arm to touch her face. Her nose and both of her eyes were swollen. She fingered several cuts and bandages. Her stomach ached and her right leg throbbed. Her chest felt as though someone jumped on it each time she inhaled.

She closed her eyes.

"Liza?" She didn't recognize the voice.

She opened her eyes and saw a short, middle-aged man with thinning brown hair and small rectangular glasses. "Yes?"

"My name is Dr. Allison." He reached over and placed his hand on her left shoulder.

Liza studied him but said nothing.

"Do you know where you are?"

Liza blinked her eyes a few times. "A hospital?"

"Yes, that's right. You're in St. Francis Hospital."

"Why?" Liza cleared her throat.

"You don't remember?" Dr. Allison grabbed a chair and set it beside Liza's bed. He sat next to her.

"No." Perspiration beaded on her forehead.

Dr. Allison pursed his lips together. He took a deep breath and let it out slowly. "Late last Friday night, you were involved in an automobile accident. You were brought here, and I've been your doctor. I must say, you've certainly given us a scare."

"An accident?" The haze in Liza's memory began to clear.

"Quite a severe accident. You were lucky. I believe your seat belt saved your life."

Liza searched her mind, trying to recall any of the events from that night. "I don't . . . I can't seem to . . . I'm not sure—"

"There's no need to push yourself, Liza. You don't need to dredge up all of the details right now. You've been unconscious since the accident and you've had two surgeries to repair the damage to your arm. We also had to remove your spleen. The internal bleeding has stopped. You've suffered a serious concussion. You don't have a brain injury, but we're going to keep watching you. You also have lacerations on your face and leg."

Liza gazed at her right arm. She'd noticed the bandage before, but she hadn't realized that thin metal pins stuck out of the dressing.

Liza sighed. "Why are these things in my arm?"

"During the accident, your upper arm was crushed. We've put pins in your bone to hold it together, and we've started a skin graft. You'll need to work with your arm so that the muscles don't atrophy." Dr. Allison gently moved her arm.

"This is my shooting arm. I'm planning to play basketball this fall, probably for Oak University. I've been offered a place on the team and a scholarship." She coughed a few times.

Dr. Allison remained silent. His gaze shifted as he caught a glimpse of a nurse in the doorway. "Excuse me for a moment."

Liza figured her arm would heal in the next two months because the last time she'd broken a bone, it took less than two months to heal. Although her injury seemed a bit more serious now, she'd need to practice hard this summer so she'd be ready for the upcoming season.

Dr. Allison stepped next to her bed. "I'm sorry about that, Liza. Are you comfortable?"

Liza cleared her throat. "I guess, considering. Was I by myself in the accident?"

"No."

"Was my family with me?"

"Your mother and your brother were in the car with you."

"Not my dad?"

The doctor shook his head. "No. He wasn't in the car."

"Oh. I can't really remember."

"You may never recall the accident. That's normal."

"Where's my mom? Jason? Are they here in the hospital?"

Dr. Allison's face paled and he frowned. Liza assumed from his expression that her mother and Jason had been hurt as well and were somewhere in the hospital.

"Where are they? I want to see if Jason—"

"Liza," Dr. Allison cut in, "your father is waiting outside to see you. Can he come in?"

Liza turned her head. She wasn't sure if she wanted to see him or not. She sensed that she was angry with him, but couldn't pinpoint the exact reason why she was mad because her thoughts were still fuzzy.

"Liza? Your father wants to speak with you. He's been waiting for you to regain consciousness." Dr. Allison seemed to be pleading with her.

"Go ahead and send him in, I guess."

Her father stepped through the doorway and approached her bed. "Liza."

"Dad."

"How are you feeling? I've been so scared that you wouldn't wake up." He reached for her left hand and grasped it. He pulled in a chair close to her bed and sat down.

"I've been better," she said.

Liza stared at her father. He appeared to be so emotional, almost overwrought. He usually wasn't so dramatic.

"Dad?"

He buried his head in her bed.

"What is it?" Liza gazed at the top of her father's head. A cold chill began to envelop her. "Dad? The doctor said Mom and Jason were with me in the accident. Where are they? Are they in the hospital?"

He said nothing, but wept out loud.

"Come on, Dad. What's going on?" The cold sweats started at the back of her neck and soon covered her face.

Still, he said nothing. He grasped Liza's left hand even tighter.

A feeling of dread encompassed her. "I mean it. Tell me what's going on."

Her dad raised his head a few inches. "Your mom . . . Jason . . . they . . . the rescuers tried everything, they tried all they could . . ."

"What're you saying?" Perspiration dripped down her forehead and the loud, rhythmic beating of her heart pounded in her ears.

He lifted his head high enough to peer at Liza. "Mom and Jason died at the scene." His head fell to the bed, his shoulders rising and falling.

Numbness enshrouded her. What had he said? Her mom couldn't be dead. Jason couldn't be dead. How could she be alive and both of them be dead? It must be a mistake. Her dad must be confused and not know what he's saying.

"No, Dad, they're fine. I'm sure they're somewhere in this hospital. Jason's going to make everyone feel all sorry for him. You go and find them so I can see them."

Her father raised his head and looked directly at Liza. "Mom and Jason are gone."

Liza shook her head. "No. That can't be true. I don't believe it. We were just—"

The walls of the room closed in on her as she struggled to breathe. Panic gripped its fingers around her neck and squeezed tight.

A deep, piercing scream, originating from the outer extremes of her body and reverberating through every minuscule part, projected itself from her mouth.

"Please, stop screaming!" her dad pleaded.

The scream transformed into a moan and brought three nurses to her room.

Dr. Allison entered the room and gave her an injection. Liza continued to groan and murmur to herself until she succumbed to sleep.

Chapter Thirty-One

Liza awoke to her dad sitting by her bedside, his eyes red and swollen. He'd become part of her horrible nightmare, and she wrestled to make herself wake up. When she'd had other frightening dreams, all she had to do was concentrate and tell herself to wake up.

Her dad gazed at her. "How are you feeling?"

"I feel kind of weird, like I'm floating or something." *Must be part of this same awful dream.* "Wake up. Right now. Wake up."

"Liza?"

"Wake up. Now." She pinched herself.

"What are you doing?" He crinkled his nose.

"You're part of this terrible dream and I'm done with it. I want to wake up. Right now."

"Liza," he stroked her head, "this isn't—"

"Oh, yes, it is. It's one of the most realistic dreams I've had, but it's definitely a dream."

"Liza—"

"Dad, really. I feel all weird because I'm about to wake up and forget about this whole nightmare."

"The doctor gave you some medication because of your reaction earlier. That's why you feel so strange . . . not because it's a dream."

Liza's skin tingled. She glanced around the room while she blinked her eyes. "No. It can't be—"

"It is."

Liza's head fell back forcefully against her pillow. The accident hadn't been a horrific nightmare, but was, in fact, her new reality. "How can it be true?"

Her dad said nothing.

"What will we do without Mom and Jason? It doesn't seem real. I keep going over in my mind what happened and—"

Her dad placed his hand on hers. "Stop thinking about it, Liza. It will only make the hurt even more unbearable—like someone's plunged a knife in your heart and you can't remove it. You can't breathe or think or do anything but ache." A tear fell down his cheek.

"But I want to know what happened. I can't seem to remember. Why did we have the accident? What happened? Why were we even in the car?"

He reached his hand up and caressed her cheek.

She leaned into her father's hand. "Mom always touched my cheek like that. She'll never do that again. Never," she whimpered.

Her dad once again buried his head next to her and sobbed.

*   *   *

The next morning Liza stared out the window, trying to digest the excruciating truth. A portly older woman with bleached blonde hair came in. "Hello, Liza," the woman said in a slight southern accent.

When Liza didn't answer, the woman said, "I'll be your nurse today. My name is Kathryn, but people call me Kit. If you need anything, you can push that button over there and I'll come a runnin'. Are ya ready for breakfast?"

Kit pulled out a thermometer and placed it in Liza's mouth. Liza gagged.

Kit left the room and then returned with a plate. She placed it on the table next to Liza's bed. "Try to eat something. You need your strength."

Liza closed her eyes and tried to remember details of the accident. Her memory was foggy, but she concentrated on recalling the events immediately prior to the wreck. Though it was agonizing, she wanted to understand what had happened and why. She wanted to remember.

Kit interrupted her thoughts as she entered the room and said, "You have some visitors."

Liza glanced at the door and watched Mr. Reynolds and Kyle enter the room. They were both dressed in white shirts, ties, and dress pants.

"I'm so sorry about what's happened, Liza. What can we do to help you?" Mr. Reynolds asked.

Liza shrugged.

"We wanted to come by so you'd know we were thinking of you," Mr. Reynolds said.

Liza's reply caught in her throat.

"We don't want to keep you from your rest. Please, know that you will be in our prayers." Mr. Reynolds rested his hand on Liza's shoulder.

"Dad, can I stay for a little while?" Kyle implored.

"Is that okay with you, Liza?"

She nodded.

"Thanks, Dad," Kyle said.

Kyle sat on the chair next to her bed. No words were exchanged for some time. Kyle finally broke the silence. "I am so sorry about what's happened."

Liza gave a slight nod.

"Can I do something for you?"

"Yeah."

"What?"

"Rewind time."

Kyle gazed at the floor.

"Then, no. You can't do anything for me."

After several minutes, Liza said, "What hurts so much is that

I'll never see them again. I can't tell them how much I love them, even Jason. If I had another chance. If I could only . . ."

"You can be with them again."

"I know you believe all that stuff, but I don't." Liza wiped the tears from her cheeks.

"You'll see your mom and Jason again someday. This isn't the end."

"I wish I could believe that, but . . ."

"Do you trust me?" Kyle's eyes were soft and inviting.

It seemed an odd question. Liza answered, "Yeah. I guess."

"If ever you've believed anything I've said to you, believe this. You will see them again. Families don't end with death."

Liza let out a long sigh. She wiped at her eyes again. "You're all dressed up." She blew her nose.

Kyle seemed uncomfortable as he shifted his weight in the chair. "I'm on my way somewhere, that's all."

"Where?"

Before Kyle could respond, a tall, muscular policeman with black hair entered the room. "I'm sorry to bother you, Ms. Compton, but I have to ask you what you remember about the accident."

Kyle moved out of the officer's way. Liza stared at him for a few seconds and said, "I don't remember much. In fact, I'm not really sure what happened."

"Apparently, from the accident scene, you were traveling down the pass toward the city when another driver approached your vehicle and collided with your automobile. Do you remember any details?"

Liza searched the hidden pockets of her mind for any memories of the accident but still could recall nothing. "We were driving back to the city?"

"Yes."

"From the . . . cabin."

"We think the other driver may have fallen asleep and drifted into your lane."

Liza closed her eyes briefly. She said, "Did you ask him why he killed my family?"

"The other driver was a woman. She wasn't wearing her seat belt, and she died about an hour after she reached the hospital. We're still waiting for a toxicology report, but all indications point to her simply falling asleep at the wheel."

Liza's body throbbed. She couldn't breathe.

"I'm sorry for your loss. I understand the services are scheduled for this morning."

"This morning?" Liza glanced at Kyle. The agony swallowed her as she comprehended the policeman's words.

"Officer, can you come back later?" Kyle asked.

"I think I have all of the information I need. I'm sorry, Ms. Compton, I truly am." The officer turned and left the room.

Kyle gazed into her eyes and said, "I'm so sorry."

* * *

"Seems like a real nice young man," Kit said as she checked the IV bag and scribbled on her clipboard.

"Huh?"

"The one that was here earlier. Handsome. And very polite."

Liza gave a nod.

"I'm sure sorry about your loss. I'm hopin' you'll be outta here real quick."

"I want to leave right now."

"Well—"

"Please. Can you help me?"

Kit shook her head. "I—"

"You don't understand. I have to go. I have to see them. Please."

Kit looked at her with a questioning expression.

"I have to say good-bye. I'll never see them again. I'm begging you. Please?"

"What are you talking about?"

"I have to find out where they are. I want—"

"Are you talking about the services for your mom and brother?"

"Yes. I have to go."

"I'm sorry, but you're in no position to leave. Your injuries are too—"

"I don't care about me. Don't you get it? My mom and brother—I have to go." Liza's tears streamed down her face and dampened her gown.

Kit placed her hand on Liza's shoulder.

Liza stared at Kit. "Why didn't I die with them? Why did I have to survive? What's the point?"

"I don't know much about these things, but I believe in God and I believe He'll take care of ya."

Liza rolled her eyes. "Yeah right. Like how He took care of my mom and Jason?"

"You still have your father, don't ya? That's a blessing." Kit smiled.

"A blessing? Are you kidding? In a few days he'll be back at work like he always is." Work. Like he always is. The words pounded in her mind. Something clicked. She covered her mouth. Her memory fog started to clear as she recalled bits and pieces from that dreadful night.

Suddenly, Liza realized a painful truth. Her chest rose and fell rapidly as she contemplated this realization. She closed her eyes and shook her head as the fury inside of her mushroomed.

"What is it?"

Through labored breaths Liza said, "We were at the cabin waiting . . ."

"Yes?"

"My dad. This is his fault. All of it. How could I have forgotten?"

"What do you mean?"

"He didn't . . ." She choked back the tears.

Kit rubbed Liza's hand. "You've been through an awful ordeal, especially for such a young girl. You need time to come to terms with all of this."

"I will never come to terms with any of this." She wiped at her nose. She turned her head and tried to bury her face in her pillow. It wasn't real. How could it be? This had to be a nightmare. It had to be.

Chapter Thirty-Two

"You've got to take this medication. The doctor has ordered it," an unfamiliar nurse barked.

"I couldn't care less what the doctor ordered. I don't want anything else from anyone here. I'm sick of all of you. Get out of my room and leave me alone."

"But it's my job."

"You know what? I don't care about your job. My mother's dead. My brother's dead. I'm stuck in this hospital with pins coming out of my arm, and you think I care about your job? Get out. Get out and don't come back."

"This attitude of yours won't go over well, you know. I'm only doing my job. I'm trying to help you."

"Don't care."

"I'm not going to force you to take pain medication. If you want to be in unnecessary pain, I guess that's your choice. You can call for me when you change your mind." The nurse turned around and stomped out of the room.

Liza laid her head back and breathed in deeply to try to counteract the pain in her arm.

A few moments later, she recognized Coach Anderson's voice. "Liza? May we come in?"

Tamika, Brittany, and Sara followed the coach into the room. They all walked slowly to her bedside.

"We brought you some of your favorite candy. You know, chocolate anything," Tamika said.

Sara placed a large white stuffed bear on the end of Liza's bed. Brittany smiled and said, "How's it goin'?"

"You've had us worried. I'm so glad to see you're doing better," Coach Anderson said.

"Better?"

Coach Anderson bent down. He came in close and said in a whisper, "Liza, I am so, so sorry about your mother and Jason."

Tears welled up in his eyes as his warmth settled on her. Coach Anderson hugged her as best he could.

"Thank you," Liza said as Coach Anderson pulled away.

"The girls and I have been waiting to see you. They've all been concerned about you."

Tamika, Sara, and Brittany took turns hugging Liza.

"We all feel so bad," Tamika said.

Sara twisted her hair between her fingers. "English hasn't been the same without you. Mr. Snyder assigned a research paper on Monday and it's already due tomorrow. How can he expect us to do all of that work in only five days? He's so—"

Coach Anderson cut in. "Is this a good time for a visit?"

Liza brightened. She hadn't realized how much she missed her teammates until they walked through the door. It was a welcome relief to see familiar faces that had no connection to her current state. "How are things at school? Tell me everything."

"As if the research paper wasn't enough, Mr. Snyder also gave us this huge project to work on for the rest of the year," Sara said.

"About what?" Liza asked.

"We have to choose a book and write about how it's influenced us and then come up with other ways to show its importance in our lives. Whatever."

"I'd hate that. I hate reading," Tamika said.

After a few more comments, Coach Anderson said, "We don't want to tire you, but we wanted you to know that we love you and we're here for you."

"Wait. I'm not tired. I want to hear more," Liza said.

"The doctor told us to limit our visit. We better listen to him," Coach Anderson said.

"You don't have to listen to the doctor. Really. Stay for a while."

"I'm sorry, but we promised we wouldn't stay too long." Coach Anderson patted her left shoulder. The girls each waved as they left the room.

Liza stared out the window. While she visited with the coach and the girls she'd been able to think about something else, even if it was only momentary. Now, as she lay in the empty room, reality hit her hard.

She'd wanted things to change with her family, but never in her wildest imagination did she think something like this would happen. She'd wanted her father to pay more attention to her, and she'd wanted her family to be like it used to be. She hadn't wanted everything to change so drastically that she may not even survive it.

*   *   *

A few hours later, Liza awoke to the sour odor that indicated it was dinnertime. The only thing worse than the smell of hospital food was its taste.

Dr. Allison walked in and sat in a chair beside her bed. "How are you feeling, Liza?"

Liza stared at him. What a ridiculous question.

"How is your arm? Any pain?"

Liza slowly blew out a breath. "A little."

"I hear you wouldn't take any medication."

"I guess I was a little harsh on that nurse."

"Tell me how your arm feels."

"I don't know. It looks like it's a mess to me, but that doesn't matter as long as I can get to my practices this summer and get ready for the season." She glanced at her arm and then at the doctor. "How much longer until my arm is normal again?"

Dr. Allison cleared his throat. "I'm not sure you understand the gravity of the injury to your arm."

Liza's eyes grew wider. "You said I was lucky."

"Yes. You were extremely fortunate to survive such an accident. However, the injury to your arm is extensive."

"What're you saying?"

"Has your father been by to speak with you today?"

"Nope. Why?"

"Well, I'd prefer that a family member be present while we discuss your injuries."

"My family's gone. Remember?"

"Your father—"

"You can't depend on him, I ought to know. Just get on with it."

Dr. Allison appeared to be having an internal discussion. "Very well. Liza, as you know, your arm was crushed in the accident. We have placed some pins to hold it together, but we expect a long recovery."

Liza blinked her eyes several times. "How long?"

"Possibly years. In fact, you may never recover full use of your arm."

"But this is my shooting arm. It has to work. My place on Oak's team, my scholarship. You can't be serious."

Dr. Allison removed his rectangular-shaped glasses and rubbed his eyes. He placed his hand on his chin. "Liza, I don't believe you'll ever play basketball again. I'm not sure that you'll even be able to use your fingers as you did before the accident."

Liza swallowed hard. She didn't know what to say. She was stunned. Sadness and fear paralyzed her. She'd lost her mother and brother, and now, she'd lost the one thing that made her who she was. How could this happen?

"This is a lot for you to take in. Perhaps we should continue this conversation another time when your father can be present." Dr. Allison replaced his glasses and smoothed his hair.

Liza stared at the wall. Basketball? How could she lose basketball on top of everything else?

Dr. Allison stood. "I'll come back later and see how you're doing. We'll need to schedule you for another surgery in the next few days."

Liza said nothing. She barely noticed him as he left her room.

The tears snaked down her cheeks. This was too much. It was bad enough that her mom and Jason had been ripped from her. Now basketball had been yanked out from under her too. What had she done to deserve this?

She began to sob. Her life was over. She had nothing left and only one person was to blame—her dad. He was responsible for all of this. He might as well have pushed their car over the cliff. He'd not only destroyed their family, he'd also ruined the rest of her life.

How could she possibly go on? All she knew and cared about had been snatched away from her, and she was left with nothing.

Why did she survive only to have nothing left?

She felt drained, physically and emotionally. She shut her eyes and started to drift off, hoping that in sleep she might find some comfort or at least escape the razor-sharp pain that engulfed her.

A familiar voice interrupted her plan.

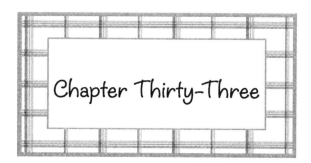

Chapter Thirty-Three

"Liza?"

Before she even opened her eyes she said, "Kyle."

"How's everything? Sorry, lame question."

"Yeah," Liza's lips quivered.

"What's going on?" Kyle sat on the edge of her bed.

"I've lost basketball."

"What?"

"My arm. I'll never play again." Liza's voice caught on each word.

"Is that what the doctor said?"

"Yep, pretty much. I guess you could say I've lost everything. There's nothing left." Liza blew out enough breath that her limp bangs moved slightly.

"I know it seems bad, but there is always hope. You still have your dad and maybe—"

"My dad?" Liza straightened her blanket. "This whole mess is his fault. I don't want to work things out with him. I hate him."

"You don't mean that."

"Oh yes, I do. If he'd come to the cabin. If he'd kept his

word. Just this one time, if he'd done what he promised, none of this would've happened."

Kyle said nothing for a few moments. Softly he said, "You can get on with your life, Liza. Things can work out."

"You are always so up, always so cheerful and happy, but there are some things that can't be the way you see them. Not everything works out."

"It does if you have faith. Heavenly Father loves you, and He can help you through this. I know He can."

"Please, don't go there. Not now. Don't give me any religion right now."

"I only want—"

"You want me to believe the same things you do, but I don't. I don't even know what faith is and I don't want to know. My life isn't worth anything anymore. I've lost everything that's ever mattered to me, and you can't possibly understand."

"I'm sorry. You're right. I can't understand what you're feeling, but I do understand having faith even when things seem hopeless."

"Yeah, well, I'm not interested in any Mormon talk."

Kyle wore a disappointed expression. "I guess I better get going. I have a chemistry test tomorrow." He gave a wave and left the room.

Liza shook her head. Why couldn't she give up on life without Kyle interfering? She had every right to be depressed and hopeless. He was obviously disappointed in her. She could add that to the list of her miserable life.

Chapter Thirty-Four

"What day is it?" Liza asked.

"It's Monday, the twenty-second." Kit said.

"I've been in here for ten days?"

Kit nodded and checked Liza's vitals. "The doctor said your surgery went well this morning."

"I guess." Liza gazed out the window into the darkness. Emptiness consumed her. Her surgery had gone well, and, if she was lucky, she'd possibly get more use out of her arm. So what? It didn't mean she'd play basketball. What did it matter? She'd never play competitive basketball again.

The unbearable pain left by the deaths of her mom and her brother was still hot and raw. Her life had taken such a dramatic twist in the last ten days. It was difficult to make sense of any of it.

Now, though she hated to admit it, she yearned for her father. She wasn't sure why, but she felt an uncontrollable urge to see him. Her feelings confused her. How could she want to see the one person responsible for all of the grief and despair she now felt? She couldn't possibly still love him, could she? How could she when he'd so obviously deserted her yet again? While that was his expected behavior before the accident, somehow, she'd mistakenly thought he'd make more of an attempt to see her as she lay broken in the hospital.

If only he'd come to the restaurant like he promised. If only he'd met them at the cabin. If only . . .

She wanted to wallow in her self-pity. She felt justified in her misery. Everything she'd planned—gone. Everything she'd hoped for—vanished. Life held nothing more for her, and she wanted to be left alone to sink lower and lower into her depression.

"You have a visitor waiting to see you," Kit said.

"Who?"

"That handsome young man with blond hair."

"Kyle."

"He's been waiting for you to recover from your surgery." A warm sensation covered Liza. Even after she was so rude to him the other night, he'd come back and even waited for her to recover. She'd expected him to never want to see her again.

"There are some flowers and other cards out on the nurses' desk. I can bring them in," said Kit.

Liza nodded.

A short time later, Kyle walked in with an enormous vase filled with various flowers including red roses and red carnations. Blue ribbons adorned the vase so she knew who sent the flowers. "I think these are for you, Madame," Kyle said. He bowed.

Despite her somber mood, the corners of her mouth turned up slightly. "Can you read the card?"

" 'We miss you and want you back here suffering in school like us.' Must be from those basketball nerds," Kyle said with a grin.

"Excuse me?"

"Kidding, of course. Coach Anderson signed it too." Kyle placed it on a shelf opposite Liza's bed.

Liza laid her head back and attempted pleasant, light conversation. "How were your morning classes?" she asked with a smile.

"Good, as far as you know," Kyle said.

She raised her eyebrow and said, "Really?"

"You got me." He shrugged. "I've been here while you were in surgery. You were pretty upset last time I talked to you, and I wanted to see how you were doing."

Liza glanced at her hand and then looked at Kyle. "I'm sorry for the way I treated you."

"Apology accepted."

They continued to visit. For the first time since she found herself in the hospital, Liza almost forgot where she was. She admired Kyle's ability to numb her pain, even if it was only temporary.

Kyle placed a Book of Mormon on the table.

She moved uncomfortably in the bed.

"I know what you said the other night about religion and faith, but I keep having this feeling that I need to bring this to you." Kyle glanced at the ground. "I hope you don't think it's weird, but I've been praying about how to help you."

"You have?"

"You were right. I can't begin to understand your pain, but I know who can."

"Who?"

Kyle peered into Liza's eyes. "The Lord."

Goose bumps erupted on Liza's body, and a warm feeling settled on her chest.

"He understands all of our pain." Kyle pushed the book closer to her. "I marked some scriptures for you to read."

Liza stared at the book. She hadn't thought much about the Book of Mormon or the Church since the accident. It was too agonizing to think about anything, but seeing the book triggered memories of conversations she'd had with her mom. She reached over and gently placed it on her lap. She opened it.

"I know this book is from the Lord because I've prayed about it. And I know that He can help you heal, if you'll trust Him." Kyle's eyes communicated his sincere belief. He reached over and placed his hand on hers.

She felt the physical attraction, but it was more than that. His touch conveyed something beyond mere magnetism. It was the same peace she experienced when he and his dad visited before the accident. It was the same sensation she had when she stayed awake in her parents' bed reading passages from the Book of Mormon. Maybe he was right about healing. Maybe the Book of Mormon could offer her some answers or at least some comfort to ease the sharp, jagged pain that had become her constant companion.

Kyle glanced at his watch. "I better let you get some rest." He left the room.

Liza thumbed through the pages of the Book of Mormon and found the passages Kyle had marked for her.

She read, "Behold, there is a time appointed that all shall come forth from the dead" (Alma 40:4). She laid the book down in her lap as she considered the words "come forth from the dead." That seemed pretty clear cut. She continued to read. "Therefore, there is a time appointed unto men that they shall rise from the dead" (Alma 40:9). She studied the other passages about how the spirit and the body would be reunited again after death and that everyone would be resurrected and live again.

If that were true—really true—then her mom and Jason would live again. Maybe death wasn't the end. She closed the book and cradled it to her chest. She wanted to believe in those words. She wanted to believe she'd see her family again, but she was afraid.

Chapter Thirty-Five

£iza slowly opened her eyes. Someone was in her room, sitting next to her bed.

"Hello, Liza."

"Dad." Liza cleared her throat.

"How are you?" His voice was forced. His shirt was wrinkled and his hair wasn't combed. His eyes were red and so was his nose.

Liza blinked her eyes several times. "Fabulous, how about you?"

Her dad glanced at the ground and said, "I'm sorry I haven't been here for a while. I—"

Liza cut in, "Don't sweat it, Dad. I'm used to it."

"Let me finish. I can't seem to come to terms with all of this. I feel like I'm walking in a fog and I can't see in front of me."

"I feel real bad for you." She rolled her eyes.

"I don't understand—"

"Me either."

"If only you guys hadn't tried to drive back to the city."

The crystal clear memories poured in her mind. "Yeah. If only."

"Whose idea was it anyway?"

Liza's heart pounded in her chest as she recalled trying to convince her mom to stay at the cabin. "Seriously though, if you want someone to blame, Dad, look in the mirror."

"What do you mean?"

"Don't you get it? This is your fault."

"My fault?" He rose from the chair. "How could this be my fault?"

Her voice cracked as she said, "You were supposed to meet us at the restaurant."

"I know that, but I called and said I had to finish some paperwork."

Liza struggled to remain calm, but her anger roiled. Her internal volcano was about to rival Mt. Vesuvius and, like the city of Pompeii, everything in sight would be covered in red-hot lava. "Like usual, your job got in the way. You said you were going to change. You promised. We waited and waited at the cabin for you."

"I still had some work to do. I didn't know you'd be driving back." Her dad paced in front of her bed. He ran his fingers through his hair.

Liza's voice took on an icy edge. "Mom was too worried about you. Jason and I both tried to convince her to stay at the cabin and not go looking for you because we knew you were working. We knew you were blowing us off and that you are nothing but a liar."

"I—"

"Mom believed that you wanted to change. She believed that you'd come like you said, and when you didn't show, she thought you needed help." Liza's eyes burned.

"Liza—"

"But you were at work." Liza's chest heaved with each breath. "Ever since we moved here, your career has been more important to you than our family. I tried to make you see that. I tried to talk to you. Mom tried to talk to you, but you wouldn't listen. You made empty promises to satisfy us. You never planned to change anything."

"That's not true."

"Now you've sacrificed our family forever and there's no going back. This is your fault. Yours. No one else's."

"Please, wait—"

"You might as well have killed them yourself. I never want to see you again. I want you to leave and never come back. You're not my dad. You're as dead to me as Mom and Jason." It was out. Her words hung low and heavy like a bulging storm cloud. He deserved it, though, because this was his fault and she would never forgive him, not this time. So much for her yearning desire to see him.

"This isn't my fault." Her father staggered over to a chair, mumbling to himself. Liza turned her head and stared out the window. Hate wasn't strong enough. She despised him. She never wanted to see him again. Ever.

Chapter Thirty-Six

Liza surfed through channels on the hospital television, trying to find something to erase her memories of the ugly confrontation she'd had with her father the day before. Kit, her regular nurse, peeked her head in the door and said, "Liza? There's a man here to see ya."

"Tell my so-called dad that I don't want to see him and that's it. Tell him to go away and never come back."

"It isn't your father. He said his name is Steven Marcus."

Liza coughed a few times. "Oh, tell him to come in." Maybe this would be good news, finally. Maybe he wanted to let her know that her space on the team was reserved for her, and as soon as she was healed, she'd play for Oak. Maybe everything wasn't lost after all and she'd regain basketball, despite what Dr. Allison said. Maybe there was still hope.

Liza smoothed her hair as Mr. Marcus entered the room. He had a pleasant smile, but it seemed obligatory.

"Hello, Liza. I'm glad to see you're doing better." He nodded.

"Thank you. It's nice to see you." She pulled at her blanket.

"I wanted to stop by and see you in person. I'm so sorry about your loss." He took a few steps closer to her bed.

"Thank you." She bit her lip.

"What is your prognosis?"

"You mean, can I play basketball?"

"Something like that."

"Dr. Allison tells me I'll never play basketball again, but . . ." A lump grew in her throat. "If you'll give me a chance, a little time . . . I can play again. Really."

Mr. Marcus clicked his tongue. "I see."

Awkward silence choked the oxygen out of the room. Liza blinked away her tears.

"I feel bad having to do this. It isn't a fun part of my job, but I'll have to withdraw my offer. I'm truly sorry, Liza." He sounded sincere, but each word felt like an ice pick plunged into her chest.

"Can't I have more time?"

"I'm sorry, but my hands are tied on this. We have other players—"

"I understand." She pursed her lips together.

"If there was any chance . . ."

Liza nodded.

"I'm sorry." Mr. Marcus gave a faint smile. He turned and exited the room.

So it was final. She'd truly lost everything. Her chance to play for Oak was gone. Her mom and Jason were gone. What was left? Nothing. Absolutely nothing.

Chapter Thirty-Seven

Liza spent the next several days enduring visits by different specialists who assured her she may regain some use of her arm. She didn't care. If she couldn't play basketball, her arm didn't serve any real purpose.

Each day dragged on as if it would never end. Her father had tried to see her, but she refused to see him. She hadn't seen Kyle for several days and wondered why.

Kit walked into her room. "How ya feeling today, hon?"

Liza didn't respond.

"You haven't touched your breakfast. How 'bout eatin' some?"

"Not hungry."

"Rumor has it you're not eatin' too much. You need to get your strength." Kit smiled.

"Why?"

Kit tilted her head to the side and said, "I'll see if the kitchen can whip you up something." She left the room.

A few minutes later, Dr. Allison walked in. "Liza?"

Liza glanced at him and then out the window. "Yeah?"

Dr. Allison pulled a chair next to her bed. "Since your last surgery went so well, I think you can start rehab. I'm pleased with your progress."

Liza looked at the doctor. "Will I be able to play basketball this fall?"

Dr. Allison stared at Liza for a few moments. "We've talked about this. I'm sorry, but right now, we're focused on you regaining the most use of your arm. Basketball—"

Liza cut him off. "I know. Never mind. It doesn't matter anymore." Liza gazed out the window.

"I don't want you to give up, Liza. This surgery went well, and it's possible you'll have almost full use of your arm within a year. This is very good news."

"Is it?"

"You could have died in that accident."

"But I didn't. I'm stuck here with no family, no future, and nothing to live for."

"That isn't at all true. You have your whole life ahead of you," Dr. Allison said.

Liza gazed at Dr. Allison. "What life? You mean the one without my mom, without my brother, without basketball, without my scholarship? You mean the one without anything I've planned?"

"I'm going to send someone in to talk with you. Would that be okay?" Dr. Allison leaned in close to her.

"Let me guess. You're going to send in a shrink. Now I'm a mental case too?" Liza rolled her eyes.

Dr. Allison stood. "You've been through an incredible trauma. You're trying to deal with an overwhelming tragedy, and maybe it would help to speak with someone. Dr. Lindon is excellent and easy to talk to."

Liza said nothing more to Dr. Allison. She shut her eyes and lost herself in her thoughts. She wished she were with her mom and brother, wherever that was. Dr. Allison's footsteps faded as he left the room.

Maybe, if she concentrated hard enough, she could join her mom, somehow, some way. That seemed to be the only solution to her miserable life.

Chapter Thirty-Eight

"He's here again. Won't you let him come in, even for a minute?" Kit asked.

Liza sighed. "I've told you at least a thousand times over the last week: I don't want to see him. Isn't anyone listening to me?"

"He's still your daddy." Kit walked near the bed.

"I don't care. It's his fault that I'm in here. I don't want to see him."

Kit said in a soft voice, "Ya know, we can fix your body, but we can't fix your soul."

"Huh?"

"You're hurt a lot worse inside than outside. Ya need to forgive him, Liza. Isn't that what Dr. Lindon told you?" Kit leaned in closer.

"Who cares what she says? I have to hear her go on and on about something she has no clue about. She doesn't know anything about me. Besides who even asked you?"

"No one. I only want to help you. I have a daughter that's your age and I—"

"Want to be my mother? Sorry, that job was taken and now it's gone. I want everyone to leave me alone, especially Jim Compton. He had the chance to be my dad, but he gave it up and now it's too late. He can't even admit that this is his fault. I don't need or want him. Tell him to go away and never come back. He's not my father."

Kit left the room and Liza heard her speaking to someone out in the hall. Liza squeezed her eyes shut, trying to stop the tears from falling. She'd cried more since the accident than in her entire life, and she was sick of it. Despite her best efforts, though, tears trickled down her cheeks, burning her skin.

Lying in the same bed for the last two weeks had given her ample time to think. It was the one thing she didn't want to do, but she had little choice. Memories of her mom, especially the week prior to the accident, filled her mind. The despair swallowed her.

She thought of Jason and how he used to strut around the house thinking he was so cool. She recalled times they'd spent together, even the fights. What she would give to have one more argument with her brother. She refused to let memories of her dad invade her thoughts.

She thought about Mr. Marcus and his visit. What would life be like now? Where would she go? What would she do? She didn't care. She didn't want to go on. What was the point? She had nothing. She should've died in the accident. She wished . . .

Her eyelids felt heavy. Why did she have to live? Why couldn't she have gone with her mom and Jason, wherever that was? She couldn't face what lay ahead. How could she ever look at her father again, knowing everything was his fault?

The more her mind considered what was left for her, the more convinced she became that she couldn't endure it. Exhausted, she succumbed to sleep.

Without warning, her eyelids flew open. Light flooded her room, and she struggled to make sense of it. She raised her left hand to shield her eyes from the intense light but then squinted. Within the light she thought she saw someone. She couldn't tell who it was, but the goose bumps on her arm told her she somehow knew.

"Hello, honey."

"Mom?" Liza leaned up. She closed her eyes and then opened them again.

"Yes, it's me." Her mom moved closer to her bed.

"I knew it. I was right."

"What?"

Liza glanced around and recognized her bedroom. She could see the clothes she'd dropped on the floor, and her closet doors were open, exposing the mess her mother always reminded her to clean. "It was a horrible nightmare. It wasn't real. I haven't lost you. I'm so relieved it was only a dream."

"How are you feeling?" Her mom's satin voice enveloped her.

"Great, now that I've woken up." Liza shook her head from side to side. "It sure seemed realistic, though. I'm just glad to be home in my own room. I'm so happy to see you."

"Liza?"

"Yeah?"

"Things aren't as they seem."

"What do you mean?" Liza fluttered her eyelids.

"It wasn't a dream, honey."

"What?" Her voice was loud.

"The accident—it wasn't a dream." She sat next to Liza on the bed. She reached over and caressed Liza's cheek. Liza closed her eyes and soaked in the warmth of her mother's touch.

"But you're here. I can see you. I can feel you. I can even smell your perfume."

"In a way, yes."

Liza shook her head. "You're not making any sense. I don't understand."

"Let me explain." She took Liza's hand in hers. "The accident did happen, and Jason and I have crossed over to the other side."

"Other side of what?"

"Do you remember when Kyle and his father taught us about where we were before we were born, why we're here on earth, and what would happen after we die?"

"Kind of."

"It's true. Jason and I have left mortality, and we are now in a different place." Her mom smiled.

"Well, I want to come with you then."

"You can't."

"Why not?" Liza raised her head.

"Remember when we talked about how there is a plan for each of us?"

"I think so."

"The plan for your life is to live on and find happiness. There's still much ahead of you."

"Happiness? Yeah right. That's not going to happen." Liza blew out a hard breath.

"Liza, this is important. You can choose to find happiness in spite of what's happened. I know you feel overwhelmed and frightened, but you need to choose life and joy. You need to have faith and trust in God."

"I'm sorry, Mom, but I can't think of life without you and without basketball. My life is over. It's not worth it anymore."

"That isn't true. You have so much to live for. Yes, it'll be hard for a while, but you're a fighter. When you make up your mind, nothing gets in your way. Where's my determined daughter that sets her goal, goes forward, and runs over anything or anyone in her way?"

"She's gone. I think you left her on the side of that cliff."

"No, she's right here." Her mom placed her hand across Liza's heart.

"I don't know. I can't—"

"You can, Liza. Set your mind to it and then go forward. Don't waste time feeling sorry for yourself."

"But my life is ruined."

"It's not ruined, honey. It's different. View it with new eyes. Embrace the good and find the happiness that's out there. Don't settle for anything less."

"Mom—"

"There's one more thing." Her mom squeezed Liza's hand.

"What?"

"You have to stop blaming your dad for the accident." She peered deeply into Liza's eyes.

"Why? It's his fault. If he'd met us like he said—"

"That isn't fair."

"Here we go again. You're still making excuses for him." Liza rolled her eyes.

"Stop. Your father loves you. He didn't cause the accident." She squeezed Liza's hand even harder.

"He might as well have. We would've never been on the road if he'd shown up like he said."

"I only have a few more moments with you."

"What? Why?"

"I must go back."

"No, I won't let you. I need you." Liza pulled her mother close to her and bathed herself in her mom's familiar soft scent. She wanted to stay this close to her mother forever.

Her mom sat back. "Liza, you need to forgive your father. Love him. He needs you desperately, and, whether you know it or not, you need him just as much. If you look for the good in your life, you'll find happiness, but it has to begin with forgiving your dad—for everything. You won't be happy until you can find it in your heart to sincerely forgive him. Once you do, you'll find greater happiness than you can imagine. Please, Liza."

"I can't, Mom. Every time I see him I think about the accident. It didn't have to happen. I can't forgive him."

"You can, I know you can. You have the tools. Let your heart guide you and trust in God. Remember, I'll always love you and I'll always watch over you. You're my daughter, and not even death will ever change that. Someday, we'll be together again."

"Mom? Mom? . . . Mom?"

"It's okay, Liza, I'm here." It wasn't her mom, it was Kit.

Liza opened her eyes. "What?"

"You were calling out for your mother." Kit patted Liza's hand.

"Where is she? She was here a second ago. Mom?" Liza searched the room for her mother.

Kit studied her.

"Where's my mother?" The perspiration behind Liza's neck collected and moistened the pillow.

She searched the room again. What had happened? Was it a dream? Did she actually see and talk to her mom, or did she imagine it all? Was she losing her mind? Dazed, she laid her head back and closed her eyes.

Liza awoke a few hours later to Kit standing in the doorway. "Liza?"

Still confused and a bit groggy, Liza answered, "Yeah?"

"You have a visitor."

Chapter Thirty-Nine

Kyle peeked out from behind Kit's round shape. Kit said, "Can I send him in?"

"I guess." Liza glanced at the clock on the wall. Several hours had passed since her experience with her mom.

"Not the welcome I was hoping for, exactly."

"Sorry."

"No apology needed." He waved his hand. "I thought I'd stop by and see how the most famous patient from Aldrich High is doing."

Kyle's cheerful personality always had a way of making her feel better, despite everything else.

"I'm famous?"

"Absolutely. You're the hottest topic of conversation." Kyle sat in the chair at the end of her bed.

"Hmm." She fluffed her bangs.

"How're you doing today?"

Liza didn't say anything.

"I could tell you about my chemistry test."

Silence.

"What about the pep assembly?"

Nothing.

"Lunch?"

Not a word.

"The alien ship that landed on campus and kidnapped the entire cheerleading squad."

Still nothing.

"Help me out here." Kyle shrugged.

Liza, still deep in thought, said nothing.

"This is a boring conversation." He leaned the chair back. "Liza? Are you here?" He waved his hands, which caught her attention.

"Sorry. I haven't seen you for a while. Where have you been?" She regretted the words as soon as they left her mouth. Kyle wasn't obligated to come see her, and keeping track of his visits would certainly qualify her as a stalker.

"I wanted to come see you, but—"

Liza held her hand up. "It's okay, you don't have to explain anything."

"Actually, I didn't want to overwhelm you."

"With what?"

"Sometimes, I'm a little intense about the Church and the Book of Mormon. People tell me I get a little zealous and it makes them uncomfortable. With all you've had to deal with, I didn't want to make you feel weird."

"Oh."

"Is everything okay? You seem a little distracted or something."

"I'm fine."

"Are you sure?"

"Yeah."

"I'm here if you want to talk."

Liza glanced out the window and argued with herself. Should she share her experience? Was it a dream? A hallucination? If she told Kyle, what would he think? She wasn't even sure what she thought, how could she begin to explain what happened? And what if he thought she was crazy? Maybe she was crazy.

"Liza?"

Liza looked at Kyle.

"Are you sure you're okay?"

Liza nodded. She wanted to talk to someone and try to figure out what had happened to her. She wanted to understand and make sense of it, but she was afraid of what he might think, especially since she wasn't entirely certain what had happened herself.

"Have you read from the Book of Mormon?"

Kyle's question interrupted her thoughts. "Huh?"

"The Book of Mormon?"

"Oh."

"See, I'm too intense. Sorry."

"No, you're not. I read those places you marked."

"What did you think?"

"I'm not sure. I read about the resurrection. That means our bodies will be reunited with our spirits after we've died, right?"

"Yes."

"That makes it seem like there's life after death, at least according to the Book of Mormon."

Kyle nodded. "I believe there is."

"So, if it's true, that there will be a resurrection, that there's life after death—"

"We can be with our families again."

Be with her family again. Be with her mom. With Jason. Life after death. Could it be true? Really be true? "Have you ever seen anyone after they died?"

Kyle studied her. "Not exactly. Why?"

"What do you mean by not exactly?"

Kyle leaned back in his chair. He laced his fingers and placed his hands behind his head. "You're going to think this is weird."

"No. I won't."

"It sounds a little strange."

"Tell me. I want to hear it."

Kyle removed his hands from behind his head and placed his chair on all four legs. He leaned up close to Liza. "About three years ago my grandfather died."

"Oh."

"Grandpa was my pal." Kyle grinned as he nodded. "He taught me how to carve wood and how to cook over a fire. He loved to fish. I still miss him." He cleared his throat and continued. "Right after he died, I was pretty sad. My dad spent a lot of time talking to me about it. He showed me some scriptures, and then he told me to pray about it."

"And?"

"One night, I was on my knees praying to know that Grandpa was okay. After my prayer, I heard a voice. It was as clear as anything. I looked all around to see who was talking to me, but I didn't see anyone. The voice was Grandpa's."

"Serious?"

Kyle nodded. "He said not to be sad, but to be happy that he was reunited with family he hadn't seen for a long time. Then he said, 'I'll see you again.' " Kyle paused for a moment. "From that day on, I've never doubted that there's life after death, and I know that the plan of salvation is real."

A warm feeling settled on Liza. It filled the room. "You really heard his voice?"

"Yes, I did."

"Are you sure you weren't dreaming or hallucinating?"

"I'm sure."

"But you didn't see him?"

"No. I wish I could've, but I didn't. Why all these questions?"

"I'm curious. That's all." She still wasn't sure what had happened, if she'd actually seen her mom, dreamed about her, or merely imagined the whole thing. Somehow, though, a tranquil feeling encircled her as she recalled the experience, or whatever it was, and she needed to know what it meant.

Chapter Forty

"Hello, Liza," Coach Anderson said as he walked in her hospital room.

"Hi," Liza said.

The coach stepped close to her bed. "The doctor says you're doing well."

"I won't be playing basketball, but I'm getting some feeling in my fingers. I suppose you've talked to Mr. Marcus."

Coach Anderson gave a nod. "He told me he stopped by to visit. He sure feels bad about everything." He grabbed a chair, set it next to the bed, and sat.

"Yeah, he apologized and said he wished things were different. He's not the only one." She attempted a smile.

"You never know. Perhaps you'll recover the use of your arm and—"

"No, not college ball."

Coach Anderson rubbed his chin and sat back. "Have you talked to your dad lately?"

"Nope." The last person she wanted to see was the man who'd caused all of this to happen. Not only did she not want to see her dad, she didn't even want to talk about him.

Coach Anderson gazed at Liza. "You've been in this hospital for almost three weeks."

"Wow, it's been so much fun, time has flown by."

Coach Anderson's gaze intensified. "Your dad came to see me at school."

"He did?"

"Yes. He asked if I'd talk to you about seeing him."

Liza gazed at the ceiling, hoping her disinterest would signal the coach that she wasn't interested in this topic of conversation.

"He knows you're angry with him and that you blame him for the accident, but he wants to see you."

Liza looked out the window. She couldn't believe her dad had sucked Coach Anderson into pleading his case. She rolled her eyes.

"He thinks enough time has passed."

Liza sighed.

"Liza?"

"Yeah?"

"Can you look at me?"

"Sure." She stared at her coach but did not focus on him.

"He loves you."

"Uh huh."

"Really, he does. He wouldn't have come to see me unless he was desperate to talk to you. Don't you see that?"

"I meant what I said. I don't want to see him."

"You don't mean that."

"I do." Didn't she? Her mother's words urging forgiveness echoed in her ears. She shook her head. This was his fault. It was.

"He needs you desperately, and, whether you know it or not, you need him just as much." She studied her coach's mouth. "If you look for the good in your life, you'll find happiness, but it has to begin with forgiving your dad—for everything. You won't be happy until you can find it in your heart to sincerely forgive him." Liza blinked several times. It was Coach Anderson's lips that moved, but it was her mother's voice repeating the same words from the day before.

Coach Anderson asked her to reconsider her dad's request, and then he left. His visit invoked mixed feelings. Did she truly hate her dad? Or was there still a trace of love buried deep inside? Could they be a family without her mom and Jason?

Though she wouldn't say it aloud, she did, somewhere deep down, have a small, tiny, minute desire to see her dad. But for the life of her, she couldn't figure out why.

Chapter Forty-One

It was almost four p.m. Liza anticipated this time each day because a nurse wheeled her out to the terrace, where she could, for a moment, bathe in the fresh air and sunlight and allow the fragrant sea breeze to wrap around her, reminding her of life beyond the hospital. She wanted to sit on the terrace and drink in the sunshine.

She hadn't seen Kyle for a few days. She contemplated their last conversation. He was so certain she'd see her mom and Jason again. Was he right? Is that why she saw her mom? Or did she really see her? Confusion wove its way through all of her thoughts.

"Ready for the sunshine? Looks like the beginning of a beautiful weekend," Kit said. She pushed a wheelchair next to Liza's bed.

"I guess."

"It's 'bout time for you to move outta here."

Liza tucked her blanket around her lap. "Dr. Allison said something about that."

"New Hope is a nice enough place. You'll have more intensive therapy, and you'll probably be able to go home after a few weeks or so." Kit opened the glass doors and pushed Liza onto the terrace.

Home? Did that still exist, or would it only be a painful memory?

"Sure is a mighty fine day. How 'bout right here, under the arbor. The bougainvillea will shade ya."

"That's fine." Liza glanced up at the dark green leaves with deep reddish purple flowers that looked more like leaves than actual flowers.

"I'll be back in a bit."

"Thanks."

Liza laid her head back and closed her eyes. She sensed the varying degrees of sunlight that filtered through the vine. She inhaled deeply, and the smell of blooming flowers mixed with salt air filled her nose. It would be a perfect afternoon to ponder her life and her mom's words.

"Liza?"

She squeezed her eyelids. *It can't be.*

"Liza?"

It was.

"Dad." She opened her eyes.

"Can we talk?" He stepped close to her wheelchair.

"Do I have a choice?" She avoided eye contact.

Though she'd admitted to herself she had a microscopic desire to see her dad, it was far too early, and she wasn't ready to face him.

"Please, Liza."

She said nothing and stared straight ahead. Out of the corner of her eye, she could see him rub his eyes.

"You're right. I am responsible for the accident. I broke my promise to you, and, as a result, your mom and Jason are gone. You have every right to be angry. I told you I was going to be there, and I didn't keep my word. I regret it." He paused. "I'm consumed with regret. I never, ever imagined that this would happen."

Her heartbeat increased. She glanced at him sideways without moving her head, for a moment.

"I planned to drive up after I finished my paperwork, but the time slipped away from me. I know, I know, this wasn't the first time. You've been right all along. I did put my career ahead of our family. And now—"

"We have nothing left."

"I would give anything and everything if I could bring them back. I'd do anything, but I can't. I can't take it back. I can only go forward, and I need you." He paused for a few moments. "I love you, Liza. I know I haven't been there for you. I know I've missed out on things, and I know that I've hurt you. I've apologized before, but I am so truly sorry for everything." He ran his fingers through his hair and grabbed at it for a moment.

Liza said nothing.

"Is there any chance, at all, that you can forgive me?"

Liza remained silent.

"We can help each other heal. I miss them too."

Heavy silence blanketed them.

"Liza, I'm lost. Please, forgive me. I need you. Please, give us a chance to be a family."

Apparently, she wasn't going to enjoy any alone time. Her father's plea for another chance was too much, too soon. She didn't want to deal with him right now. "Take me back to my room."

Chapter Forty-Two

Liza stared at the ceiling tiles in her room. She'd already counted every tile at least a million times.

How could she possibly forgive him after what he'd done? No. Forgiveness was out of the question. She was justified. Completely justified. Right?

The door flew open.

"Hey, Liza."

"Sara."

Sara looked from side to side and behind her. "The coast is clear." She removed a paper bag from inside her jacket and put her finger to her lips. "Shh. Don't tell the cranky nurses. I brought you a shake from Gribaldi's. It's got M&Ms, extra chocolate syrup, and Snickers."

"That's my favorite."

"I know. I'm good." Sara placed the cup and a plastic spoon on the adjustable table next to Liza's bed. She maneuvered the table so it rested directly in front of Liza.

Liza started eating the shake awkwardly, using her left hand. "Mmmm. Delicious."

"I thought you'd be ready for some real food after being in here for so long."

"No kidding. The food in here is way worse than even the school cafeteria."

After a few bites of her shake, Sara sucked in her cheeks and raised her nose in the air. "Who am I?"

Liza laughed. "Mr. Snyder, of course."

"His class is so boring without you. It takes for-ev-er to get through class with him. When are you coming back?" Sara spooned a much-too-big bite into her mouth.

"I don't know. I'm moving to some other place to do physical therapy for my arm."

"So you can play for Oak?"

Liza took a deep breath.

"Oh, no. I said something wrong. I'm sorry."

Liza shook her head. "I won't be playing for Oak. In fact, the doctor said I won't be playing at all."

"Serious?"

Liza nodded.

"That's harsh. What will you do after we graduate?"

"I'm not sure I'll even be able to graduate since I haven't exactly been attending classes. It's been so fun here, I didn't want to leave."

Sara gave her a quizzical look. "Oh, you're joking."

"Yeah."

"I can get your make-up work for you. I'll bring it to you every day, and we can do homework together. You have to graduate with us."

"You'd do that? Every day?"

"Sure. You're my best friend."

Liza jerked her head back. "I am?"

"Of course. You know that."

Liza studied Sara. All this time, she'd thought she didn't have any real friends. She'd spent so much time missing her pre-Aldrich Heights life that she'd missed the fact that Sara was truly her friend. What a waste of time, feeling sorry for herself and wishing for something that she already had right in front of her.

They both took more bites of their shakes.

"I don't know what I'll do," Liza said.

"When?"

"After high school."

"Oh, yeah."

"My plans have, you know, kind of changed."

"What about your dad?" Sara dug deep in her shake. She pulled a big chunk of a peanut butter cup out and chomped on it.

"What about him?"

"What does he think you should do?"

"Who knows?"

"Haven't you talked to him?"

"Nope."

"Why not?"

"Because, it's his fault that all of this has happened."

"It is?" Sara looked bewildered.

"Yes. He was supposed to meet me and my family that night, but he never showed up."

"Really?"

"He was working. He's always working. That's why he skipped our championship game and everything else that's been important to me since we moved here."

"But he's still your dad."

"So?"

"You don't think he wanted the accident to happen, do you?"

Liza considered her answer for a moment. "No. But if he'd kept his promise to come to the cabin, things would be totally different. It's his fault that I've lost everything. You get that, right?"

Sara shrugged. "Are you going to blame him forever?"

"Maybe."

"That doesn't sound like much fun. I mean, he's still your dad and he's still here, alive, I mean. You can be a family."

"But—"

"Seems like you'd want to forget about all the bad stuff that happened before since . . ."

"What?"

"He's all you've got left. Right?"

Liza didn't respond.

"I'm sorry. I don't want to make you feel bad."

Liza wasn't successfully convincing Sara of her point. It was obvious that this was her dad's fault. How could Sara be so dense?

"I'll come by tomorrow with some assignments. I'll talk to Coach Anderson too. He can get your teachers to work things out for you. We have to graduate together."

Liza gave a nod.

"He's a great coach. I'm going to miss him when I leave for beauty school," Sara said.

Liza watched as Sara left the room. She'd misjudged her teammate. Her anger with her dad had colored her perceptions of the people around her. Maybe it was time to see things as they really were, not as she'd made them out to be.

*   *   *

The next morning, Liza awoke early. She vacillated between fear and excitement. Today she would move to the rehab center, and she didn't know what to expect. The doctor said that if all went well, she wouldn't have to stay for too long. Yet, a feeling of dread still threatened to smother her as she contemplated returning to a house without her mom and Jason.

"Here's your breakfast. I had the cook in the kitchen prepare something a little special." Kit set the plate on the table.

"You've been nice to me. I know I haven't always been the best patient. I'm sorry."

Kit stepped closer to the bed. "You've had to deal with a lot. I think you've done mighty fine."

"I don't know about that."

"Give it some time, hon."

"Sounds like something my mom would say."

"How are things with your daddy?" Kit rested her hand on Liza's shoulder.

Liza didn't say anything.

"I'm sorry. I didn't mean to pry. I'm always stickin' my nose where it don't belong. I hope it all works out for ya." Kit checked on some paperwork and then left the room.

Liza gingerly pushed the scrambled eggs back and forth with her fork. She ate a few bites of the hash browns.

"Mind if I interrupt your breakfast?"

"Kyle, I—"

"Word on the street is that they're springing you today."

"Not exactly. I'm getting out of here, but they're sending me to a rehab place called New Hope or something."

"How long will you be there?" Kyle sat on the end of the bed.

"A few weeks, maybe. It depends on how hard I work and how well my arm heals, I guess."

"I remember how hard you worked on the court. You were like a steamroller running over anyone that got in your way." Kyle imitated a steamroller. He waved his hands and said in a high-pitched voice, "Move it or I'll flatten you."

"That was a long time ago, in a lifetime far, far away."

Kyle reached over and grabbed a piece of toast. "Are you going to eat this or what?"

"Go for it." Liza paused for a moment. "Can I ask you a question?"

The door opened before Kyle could reply. Kit entered, pushing a wheelchair. "Ready for the move?"

"Uh, I think so," Liza said.

"What about your question?" Kyle asked.

"Nothing important."

Kit pushed the wheelchair close to the bed. Liza hesitated, not wanting to try to maneuver into the wheelchair in front of Kyle. Since hospital gowns don't offer the most coverage, Liza feared she'd expose too much of herself.

Kyle seemed to sense Liza's discomfort. He said, "I've got class in a few minutes. I'll come by the new place sometime." He turned around and stepped out of the room.

With Kit's help, Liza situated herself in the wheelchair. She noticed a figure in the doorway. She didn't have to guess who it was. "Can I have a few minutes?"

"You bet," Kit said as she exited the room.

Her father walked briskly to the wheelchair. He raised his hands in front of him and said, "I know you're still mad."

"I don't want to talk to you."

"Are you going to shut me out for the rest of your life?"

"Maybe."

"Can't we work this out?"

"Strange, isn't it?"

"What?"

"I begged you to talk to me so many times. I called your office. I even went to see you. I waited up night after night, but you weren't interested."

"I was—"

"Now that there's nothing to talk about, you're all for talking. The time for that is gone. Don't you get it?"

"Liza—"

"Not interested."

"But I have something to tell you."

"I don't care. Not anymore." The memory of her experience with her mom flashed in her mind, but she shut it out.

"The ambulance is here to transport Liza," Kit said as she peeked in the room.

"I'm ready to go," Liza said. Though she could see the disappointment in her father's eyes, she ignored it. "We're done here."

Chapter Forty-Three

Liza settled in her room at New Hope. She was thankful she didn't have to share a room with anyone else. The night nurse took her vitals and then turned off the light.

Liza closed her eyes, hoping that sleep would come easily.

Light rushed in her room, and she opened her eyes to see why it was so bright. Her nose registered the familiar soft fragrance that belonged to her mother.

"Mom?"

"Yes, Liza. I'm here."

"Where?" Liza shielded her eyes. When she removed her hand, her mother stood by her bedside.

"I don't understand. Is this another dream?"

Her mother gazed deeply into her eyes.

"Are you real or am I crazy?"

Her mom smiled. "Liza, you have to let go of your anger. You must forgive your father. Love him. He needs you desperately, and, whether you know it or not, you need him just as much. If you look for the good in your life, you'll find happiness, but it has to begin with forgiving your dad—for everything. You won't be happy until you can find it in your heart to sincerely forgive him. Once you do, you'll find greater happiness than you can imagine. Please, Liza."

"That's what you said last time I saw you or dreamed you or whatever."

"I'm repeating what I told you before because it's essential that you not only understand what I'm saying, but you put it into action."

Liza shook her head. "I can't do it."

"You must or . . ."

"What?"

"We can't be together. Your anger will prevent you from happiness in life and in death."

Tears welled up in Liza's eyes. "I want to be with you. Now."

"That is not the plan."

"I don't care. I miss you too much. Life is too hard."

"I know this is difficult, and I know it isn't what you planned. But, as I've said, you can still be happy. You can have a life filled with joy. But—"

Liza held her hand up in front of her. "Don't say it."

"You must forgive your dad. Only then will you be able to heal. Don't spend your life being angry with him and holding a grudge because that will only lead to misery. You both need to help each other through this."

"Mom—"

"Jason and I are okay. Don't worry about us. Focus on life and forgiving your dad."

The familiar fragrance blanketed Liza. In an instant, her mother was gone and the room was dark again.

*   *   *

A few days later, after an intensive therapy session, Liza returned to her room. After a few moments, Kyle sauntered into the room.

"How's everything?" he asked.

"Therapy is pretty rough, but my therapist is cool."

"Yeah?"

"He likes to show off the pictures of his grandkids and tell all sorts of stories about them. He sure likes his family."

"You said you had a question for me the other day."

Liza nodded.

"So?"

Liza sat up in the bed. "I want to know what it means to forgive."

Kyle raised his eyebrows. "That's a loaded question. I'm not sure I know how to answer it."

"Oh."

"Is this about your dad?"

Liza shrugged her left shoulder.

"I see."

"To be honest, I'm still mad at him for so many things. It's his fault we had the accident, even if he didn't actually cause it. But I'm getting tired of being so angry and—"

"What?"

Should she tell Kyle about her mom's visits? She still feared he'd run from her as fast as possible, but she needed to talk to someone she trusted, especially since it had happened twice. She determined to tell him and risk the consequence.

"Liza?"

"I had—"

"What?"

"I'm not sure." She squeezed her lips together.

Kyle scooted a chair close to the head of the bed and sat. "What happened?"

Liza drew in a long breath and let it out slowly. She summoned as much courage as she could and said, "I think I've dreamed something. Or maybe it really happened. I'm not sure if I was awake or asleep, or what, exactly."

"What are you talking about?"

"I don't know. Maybe I should be in a hospital for crazy people. That's where they send people who think . . ."

"Yes?"

"Never mind."

"Tell me."

"You'll think I'm weird."

"I promise I won't think that."

"It's nothing, really. Tell me about school today. Did you see Jessica?" Why did she have to speak before her brain was in gear?

Kyle cocked his head. "I want to hear what makes you think you're crazy."

Liza licked her lips.

"Will you just tell me?" He leaned up on his elbows on the bed.

After a few minutes, Liza blurted it out. "I saw my mom."

"Your mom?" He straightened in the chair.

"Twice."

"Twice?"

"See, you think I'm crazy. I can see it on your face."

"No, I don't."

"Yeah, but, I bet no one's ever told you they've seen their mother after . . . you know."

"Maybe not, but that doesn't mean I don't believe you. I think that people we've loved and lost are near us, even around us, all the time. Death isn't the end of our lives or our families. We can see them again." Kyle leaned in toward Liza. "Remember, I told you how I heard my grandpa's voice."

"But you didn't see him. I think I saw my mom. That's weird."

"I don't think so. I think it's very possible your mom came to see you to help you deal with everything."

"You really believe there's life after death?"

"I do."

"You think I'll be with my mom again? And Jason?"

"Remember we talked about the plan of salvation when my dad and I came to your house?"

"Yeah."

"Death isn't the end of us or our families."

Liza's throat tightened. She'd known Kyle for such a brief time, and yet, an undeniable *something* connected them. It wasn't just a physical attraction, but something deeper.

"It seemed so real. I could even smell her perfume. Do you think I really saw her?"

"I'm not sure, but I don't think death changed that your mom loves you."

"She told me something else." Liza played with the sheet.

"What?"

"She said I need to forgive my dad."

"Oh. So that's why you asked about how to forgive."

"Yeah, but I don't think I can forgive him. All of this is because of him. He's destroyed everything. I can't let go of the anger I feel toward him." Coldness filled the room.

"Can't or won't?"

Liza didn't say anything. Did she have a choice?

"Your life may be different than what you thought it would be, but that doesn't mean you can't be happy, unless you stay mad."

"Maybe you're right."

"Being mad won't solve anything. You have to let it go and work things out with your dad."

Liza shut her eyes. She relived the visits with her mother. After a few minutes, she opened her eyes and said, "That's what my mom said. Both times."

Kyle squeezed her hand and she felt the warmth return.

A nurse entered the room. "I'm sorry, but visiting hours are over. You're welcome to come back in the morning."

Kyle stood. "I better get going anyway. I have a lab due in chemistry."

* * *

"Do you need anything else tonight?" asked a nurse with a long black braid.

"I think I'm okay."

Liza watched the door close to her room. Therapy seemed to be going well, but what did the future hold? How could she go home to a house without her mom and Jason? And how could she live in the same house with her dad? Her anger with him had become her constant and reliable friend. Abandoning her trusted friend wouldn't be easy.

As she thought about her dad, her mom's words thundered in her ears. No matter how she tried to muffle them, they only grew louder. There must've been some reason that she saw her mom—or dreamed about her, whatever it was that had happened. Her mom specifically asked her to forgive her dad.

Was it time to discard her anger that had become so familiar and so easy to understand? Was it time to attempt a reconciliation with her dad? Truthfully, she didn't want to spend her life being miserable, and, though she hated to admit it and couldn't quite explain it, she wanted to make amends with her dad. The whole reason she'd been angry in the first place was that she felt he'd abandoned her, and she'd desperately wanted to recapture the relationship they'd had before Aldrich Heights. And Sara was right—he was still here, still alive.

Maybe she should give him another chance. Maybe she needed to concentrate on the future and stop dwelling on the past. A shiver ran up her back and made the hairs on her neck stand up. Then a warm, peaceful sensation embraced her. Suddenly, a familiar fragrance flooded her room. A scent that could only mean one thing.

"Mom? Are you here? I know you want me to forgive Dad, but I don't know how. Can you help me?"

No words came, but the fragrance still filled the room.

"Mom? I don't know what to do." She didn't know anything about forgiveness. She didn't even know where to begin. What did it really mean to forgive? It seemed out of reach, impossible.

The absence of her mom and Jason would always be a constant reminder of the part he played in the accident. How could she forget?

Chapter Forty-Four

Liza was propped up in bed watching *Smallville* when the door opened and Sara walked in.

"I've got some homework for you. Mr. Snyder, believe it or not, has actually been decent. He said that since you're still recuperating, you could read *To Kill a Mockingbird* and then answer some questions about it. He even said to tell you he hopes you can return to school before the end of the year."

"Mr. Snyder? Really?"

Sara nodded. "Amazing, huh?"

"Never would've expected that."

"I also have some assignments from Spanish." Sara reached into her backpack and pulled out a large textbook. "And I brought your American Government book. Mr. Jackson said you could write a research paper using chapters eighteen through twenty-two."

"Hmm."

"I'll bring my laptop and you can tell me what to write since it's a little hard for you to type. Then I'll take it home and print it for you and hand it in."

"Good thing I'd already taken most of my classes before this semester. I'm not sure I can even get caught up on these."

"Coach Anderson said he'd come by to help you with anything you needed."

"Sara?"

"Yeah?"

"Thanks."

"It was easy getting the stuff from your teachers."

"No. I mean, thanks for being a good friend."

"You're welcome." Sara glanced around the room. "So you've worked things out with your dad?"

"No. Why?"

"I see him every time I come to visit. I figured he was seeing you."

"Every time?"

"Yeah. He's out in the lobby right now."

"He is?"

"Do you want me to go get him?"

"No. I better get started on all this work." Liza pulled the books onto her lap.

"Okay, I'll see you tomorrow."

Sara left the room and Liza eyed the door. She could easily walk out to see her dad. But something held her back. She wasn't ready. Not yet. She needed more time.

* * *

Several days later, Liza sat in the courtyard of New Hope, reading *To Kill a Mockingbird*, when someone cast a shadow over the page.

"I read that book. Want to know how it ends?"

"Hi, Kyle. I have to read this for Mr. Snyder's class and then answer some questions. Hopefully I'll still be able to graduate."

"How's therapy going?"

"Good. I can go home at the end of the week."

"That's great."

"Is it?"

"Aren't you excited to get out of here?"

"Yeah, but I'm not looking forward to going home."

"Have you talked to your dad?"

"Not yet."

"You need to do that."

"I'm not sure how. I've been mad for so long, and I've said some horrible things to him. I don't know how to make up for that."

"Why don't you start by telling him exactly how you feel and then go from there?"

"Sara said he's been here every day, but I haven't gone out to see him and he hasn't tried to see me."

"He's probably not sure what to do, either."

"I don't want to spend the rest of my life being mad at my dad. I know that's what my mom would want, or wants. I mean, why else did I have those weird dreams or whatever? Why did I smell her perfume when I thought about forgiving my dad?"

"Because that's what will make you happy."

Liza furrowed her brows as she thought about everything. After a few minutes, she said, "But how do I actually forgive him?"

"I think if you pray about it, you'll know what to do. Prayer has helped me through hard times in my life."

She raised her eyebrows and shook her head. "Pray?"

Kyle nodded.

"But I don't know how to do that. I've never actually said a prayer before. I don't even know how to start or what to say or anything." Liza paused. She lowered her head and said quietly, "Can you . . . teach me?"

Kyle moved in close to her and sat on the bench. With a reverent voice, he taught Liza how to sincerely pray to Heavenly Father. He concluded, "Tell Him what's in your heart."

Her prayer was rough, but her anger wasn't quite as raw and white-hot after she asked for help to forgive her father.

"Feel any better?"

"A little. It still hurts, though."

"It'll take time, but things will get better. You'll see."

"I hope so. Thanks for your help."

"Anytime." He smiled.

*   *   *

After Kyle left, Liza considered their conversation and how she felt after offering a prayer. She recounted the experiences she'd had with her mother and how her mother begged her to forgive her dad. Even if she'd only imagined her mom's visits, she knew, before the accident, how much her mom wanted her to give her dad another chance.

It would be hard to start over with her dad. It would take time, a lot of it, before she could believe him again.

But she had to be honest with herself. When she peeled away all of the other feelings, an undeniable love still existed. She did want him to be in her life and she wanted to have a family. She didn't want to keep feeling dark, desperate, and hopeless.

Somehow she could do this. She didn't know how, exactly, or how long it would take, but deep down she believed she could forgive him and move on with her life. Her mother's face appeared in her mind.

*   *   *

The next day, Sara brought Liza another assignment from Spanish.

"Is my dad out there?"

"Yeah. He was sitting in the lobby, reading something."

Liza drew in a deep breath.

"Here's my laptop too. We can get started on your paper whenever you're ready, except not now."

"Why?"

"I have a date tonight. I need to go home and go through my clothes to pick out my outfit."

"Who is it?"

"Trey Williams."

Liza whistled. "Yeah, he's hot."

"I know. I did my hair for him. Do you like it?"

Liza observed Sara's light blonde streaks over deep black hair. "Looks good." Liza could finally, truly appreciate her friend's uniqueness. "Have fun."

After Sara left, Liza breathed heavily, trying to determine if she should face her dad. Was she ready? She had so much she wanted to say. How could she say it so it would make sense?

She thought about how Kyle had taught her to pray and how she felt after she prayed with him. She decided she needed as much help as she could get when she faced her dad, so she uttered a prayer. This time, the words came a bit easier and she felt a little stronger.

She stuck her feet out of the bed. *One step at a time,* she thought. She stood, grabbed a hospital gown as a robe, and opened the door. The corridor seemed to grow longer with each step. Her heartbeat increased as she neared the lobby.

She spotted her dad. He had his glasses on and seemed to be deeply involved in what he was reading. She stepped closer to him.

He glanced up once, then twice. "Liza?" He dropped his book and stood.

"I heard you were down here."

"I've been here every day, keeping track of your progress and," he glanced at the ground, "hoping you might want to see me at some point."

"Can we go out to the courtyard?"

Liza and her father walked through the glass door to the outside patio. No one else was in the area. They sat at the same bench where she'd sat with Kyle the day before.

Neither of them said anything for several minutes. Finally, Liza broke the silence. "It's been almost two months since . . ."

"Yes. I know."

"I've been angry with you for so long, I can hardly remember not being mad. Ever since you made us move to Aldrich Heights you've chosen work over our family. You worked late almost every night and even on the weekends. You tore us away from our home and friends and then deserted us."

"I know, I'm sorry—"

"I was scared you and Mom would get divorced, and I was upset that our family was falling apart. I blamed you for all of it. When you missed my games, especially my championship game, and then missed the meeting with Mr. Marcus, I snapped. I wanted to hurt you, like you'd hurt me."

Her father shifted his weight.

Liza continued, "But then, after the trip to the Stratmore, it seemed like you and Mom were going to work things out. I told Mom I wouldn't be mad at you because the most important thing to me was to get our family back to the way it used to be, before we moved. I figured if we could get back to that, but . . ." Liza paused. "The accident. I realized our family would never be back to what it used to be and you were the reason. You caused it. I didn't think I could ever see you again. Day after day, I thought about how much I hated you." Liza drew a deep breath. "I indulged myself too because I kept feeding the hate. Until—"

"Yes?"

Liza swallowed and then cleared her throat. "I had an experience."

"An experience?"

"I saw Mom. Twice, actually."

"You saw her after—"

"Yeah. At least I think I did."

"What happened?"

"She came to my room in the hospital, only it wasn't my hospital room, it was my bedroom. She was dressed all in white and she kind of floated over to me. She looked so beautiful."

"She was a beautiful woman." His voice was laced with emotion.

"Maybe it was only a dream, or my imagination, but it seemed so real."

"Did she speak?"

Liza nodded. "She said that you and I can still be a family. She told me to stop being mad at you. And . . . that we needed to help each other get through this."

Tears rolled down her father's cheeks.

"I'm not ready to jump right in. I need time, and I need space . . . and I won't make any promises."

Chapter Forty-Five

"You've made remarkable progress since you've been here. You're quite a determined young lady. I'll miss you and your friends, especially the one with the different colored hair," said Jonathan, Liza's physical therapist at New Hope.

"That's Sara."

"And, is it Kyle?"

"Yeah."

"Your boyfriend, right?"

Liza choked. "No, not my boyfriend, just a good friend."

"Your dad is filling out the paperwork right now."

Today her dad would take her home, and she wasn't sure what would happen. He'd respected her plea for time and space while at New Hope and had only visited at her request, which allowed her to have control over the situation. But now it would be just the two of them, and she'd no longer control how often or how long her father would be around. How would that make her feel? And how would she feel when she stepped into the house? Dread wound itself tightly around her.

"I'll be back in a minute. Make sure you have all of your things," Jonathan said.

Liza glanced around the room. She grabbed the Book of Mormon. She hadn't read much, but she planned to read more of it down the road.

"Here you go. I'll wheel you out to the car," Jonathan said as he patted the seat of a wheelchair.

"My legs are fine. I don't need that."

"Well of course you don't. I know that, but if I don't wheel you out, then Mrs. Penner over there will jump up and down and scream like a banshee. Nasty scene, trust me."

Liza smirked and sat in the chair. Jonathan wheeled her down the hall and to the front entrance, where her dad stood in the entryway. He guided Jonathan to the car and opened the door.

Liza rose from the wheelchair. "Thank you." She hugged Jonathan.

"Thank you for all of your work," Liza's dad said, shaking Jonathan's hand.

"Remember to do the exercises every day. You have an appointment with Dr. Hill next week."

"I remember." Liza got in the car.

Liza's thoughts tumbled in her head during the silent ride home. She hadn't been home for so long, and the last time she was home . . . She clenched her jaw as she tried to control the grief and panic that gripped her.

They approached the driveway and Liza's throat clamped shut. Her body warmed and perspiration formed on her hairline. Her dad turned off the motor and they both sat in the car for several minutes. Liza inhaled deeply and let it slowly escape through her pursed lips. She could do this.

"Maybe we should come back later," her father said.

Liza shook her head. "No. I can do it."

"You don't have to prove anything."

"I'm not."

"We can go to a hotel for a while and come back when you're ready."

"No. Sooner or later I have to face this house without them. Putting it off won't change anything."

"But—"

"I'll be fine."

One small step after another, she edged closer to the front door. Her dad stayed right behind her. She laid her hand on the doorknob, pausing for a moment. She opened the door and entered the house. She steadied herself against the door frame while tears fell from her eyes.

Her father stepped over to her. "Liza?" He put his arm around her shoulder, but she moved away.

"I'm fine."

"Let's come back later."

Liza shook her head and made her way into the living room. She sat on the couch. Her heart felt as if it were in her stomach as she gazed around the room.

"I'll bring you something cold to drink."

Liza closed her eyes and said a prayer. She'd prayed several times since Kyle taught her how to pray, and each time she prayed, she felt better. Prayer had never been a part of her life before the accident, but now it was becoming more important to her.

Her dad returned with a glass in his hand. "I've learned a few things since . . . Here you go." He handed her the glass. "It's supposed to be lemonade."

"Thanks." The cool, slightly sour drink slid over her tongue and coated her dry throat. "Tastes good."

She stiffened as her father moved closer to her. He attempted to hug her, but she didn't reciprocate.

"Liza?"

"You still have to give me room. I'm not ready to forget everything. I'm here, in the house, and that's about all I can do right now."

He moved away.

She looked at her dad and noticed the grief etched across his face. He put his hand in his pocket. "I found these on Mom's dresser." His voice caught. He cleared his throat and continued,

"She wore them when we . . . they were my mother's. Now they belong to you." He placed Grandma Compton's pearls in Liza's shaking hand.

Liza clutched the pearls to her chest and felt the strong connection to her mother. She understood, now, the importance of the pearls.

Chapter Forty-Six

During the week, Liza tried to adjust to living at home without her mom or Jason. She and her father exchanged pleasantries, but nothing more. She was thankful he respected her request for time and space.

She fixed herself a bowl of cereal and sat, huddled over the bowl, at the counter. She noticed a Book of Mormon tucked under some papers. She pulled it out and examined it. She assumed it was her mother's copy. Why was it in the kitchen?

Her father walked into the kitchen. His gaze was directed at her hands.

Liza looked down at her hands. "This must have been Mom's."

He stepped back and rubbed his chin.

"What?"

He hesitated for a moment. "It's mine."

Liza jerked her head back. "Yours?"

"Yes. Someone gave it to me."

"Who?" She sat back, stunned. She never expected her father to own a religious book.

He ran his fingers through his hair. He seemed to search for what he wanted to say. He paused for a few moments while he walked over to the love seat and sat down. "After the accident, I was in a deep, dark pit. I couldn't think of life without your mom and Jason. I couldn't get over it. I wanted to die. For days I stayed in the bedroom. I didn't eat. I didn't sleep. I wept uncontrollably. I was devastated, distraught. Like I told you, I felt like I was in a fog. After their funerals," he paused, "I couldn't do anything. Not even see you in the hospital."

He took a deep breath and continued, "I finally found the strength to come to see you and you blamed me for the accident. I was outraged that you thought it was my fault." He stared at the floor. "I couldn't believe it. Then I started thinking about that night, about all the other nights I'd stayed late at the office, or not come home at all. You were right to blame me, and I was afraid I'd lost you too." He cleared his throat.

Liza studied her father.

"Your mom was everything to me. I felt completely consumed with grief, and I couldn't imagine living anymore. My life seemed worthless, and I'd more than destroyed the relationship you and I once had. You refused to see me, and, honestly, I figured you'd be better off without me." He rubbed his temples.

Liza's heart ached as she considered what he meant. Her eyes filled with tears.

"After I spoke to you on the hospital terrace that afternoon, I came home and contemplated ending my life. Then I heard a knock. I ignored it, but then it was the doorbell. For some reason, I decided to open the door."

"Who was it?"

"A man I'd never met before. David Reynolds. He claimed he was here to help me. I didn't know what he was talking about. I tried to get rid of him and shut the door, but he insisted on coming in. I gave in and let him. He said he'd been at home, working on a project in his garage, when he suddenly felt that he needed to come over here. He dismissed it at first, but the impression came back stronger and stronger." Liza's dad got up and walked around. He continued, "I don't know how he knew I was at my lowest point, that I was absolutely hopeless. He kept telling me to not give up, that there was healing for me. He said to be patient with you. He also said someday we could all be together again. He said he felt it was imperative that I understood and believed what he was saying. It all sounded like babbling to me." Her dad sat on a barstool next to her. "He asked me to pray with him."

Liza's eyes were large with astonishment. "Did you?"

"Yes."

"You prayed?"

"We knelt down together," he pointed toward the living room, "right there. As you know, I've never been one to pray. It was strange, yet comfortable, almost familiar."

Her dad continued, "While he prayed, the warmest, most peaceful feeling filled the room and it was as if I knew God not only existed, but that He truly loved me and that I could still find happiness." He furrowed his brows. "Then, an odd thing happened."

"What?"

He hesitated a moment. In a whisper he said, "I could smell your mom's perfume."

Liza's body tingled.

"I felt like I could almost reach out and touch her. I also knew that I needed to make some drastic changes in my life, especially if I wanted to find my way back to you."

Liza watched her father intently as he continued.

"Mr. Reynolds talked to me about his visit here with you and your mom and Jason. He gave me that Book of Mormon and asked me to read in it. I've read a few passages."

Liza glanced at the Book of Mormon in her hands. "And?"

He blew a breath out. "I can't put it into words, but I felt something I've never felt before. I certainly want to believe I'll see Claire and Jason again, but I don't know. I need some time to consider everything. I don't want to make a rash decision. I'm still—"

"Yeah, me too."

"Perhaps I've been too bull-headed all of these years. I shouldn't have made your mother choose between her religion and me. I thought I was doing the right thing, but, now, it seems like I've been wrong. I don't know. What I do know is how much I need you."

Liza's eyes leaked more tears. She had no idea of the anguish that her father suffered while she'd been in the hospital. She was so focused on her feelings of grief and anger toward him that she'd never considered his feelings. She hadn't realized he was so despondent. She'd wanted to hurt him, to make him feel the same agonizing pain she felt, yet as she watched him now explain his sorrow she suddenly understood her mother's message. Her father did need her, and she needed him. She needed to see beyond her own pain and recognize that her father was suffering as much as she was. Only together would they be able to endure this tragedy and heal. Together they could be a family, as her mother said. She saw him in a new light.

"I know Mom—"

Her father inhaled deeply through his nose.

Liza smiled. "She's here."

Chapter Forty-Seven

"Adam Clawson," the announcer said. The crowd applauded.

"Courtney Collins." A short, brown-haired girl in a red cap and gown shook the hand of the principal while everyone clapped.

The announcer paused for a moment. "Liza Compton." People in the audience jumped to their feet, whistling and cheering. The thundering applause continued for almost two minutes. Classmates yelled her name and hollered.

Liza gazed out among the crowd, feeling the support of everyone in the audience. Many of those present had shared her triumph at the championship game. Now, though, her victory was different. She'd overcome something much greater than basketball opponents.

She touched the pearls she wore around her neck. In her left hand, she clutched the first place ribbon Jason had won at the Arts Center for his sketch of the volleyball player. The principal patted her shoulder. She turned to the audience and waved. At that, the crowd cheered even louder.

Liza returned to her seat and clapped as best she could for each of her remaining classmates. She whistled and yelled when her teammates received their diplomas. When it was Kyle's turn, she beamed.

After the announcer read the last name, members of the graduating class threw their caps in the air and again cheered and whistled.

Adults and youth swarmed Liza to congratulate her and wish her well. Sara rushed over sporting her new look—red hair with a black streak in front.

Since Liza's right arm was still heavily bandaged, she hugged Sara as best she could.

After the embrace, Sara said, "Is this cool or what? We're graduated. Woo hoo. No more Mr. Snyder or boring classes." She jumped up and down.

"Thanks for helping me get here. I couldn't have graduated without your help. You really are my best friend."

"No problem. We'll have to hang out this summer. Okay?"

"Sure."

"Promise?"

"Yep."

"Don't forget, party at my house tonight." Sara ran off to congratulate other classmates.

Through the crowd, Liza spotted Kyle.

He made his way over to her. "Congratulations." He gave her a hug.

"Thanks. You too."

"I've stopped by a few times at your house, but your dad said you were resting."

"It's been a hard week since I got home from New Hope. I'm just glad I could make it to graduation."

"I think everyone yelled the loudest when they heard your name."

Liza felt her face warm. "Yeah, I noticed that."

"We're all glad you pulled through."

"Thanks for all of your . . ."

"No problem. Are you coming to the beach party tomorrow to celebrate graduation?"

"Beach?" She pointed to her arm. "I'm not sure I can swim."

"Swim? Who'd ever make you swim in the cold ocean?" He grinned.

"Hmmm. I don't know."

"Oh, there's your dad over by the bleachers," Kyle said.

Liza nodded.

"Are things getting better with him?"

"Yeah, but it's still a little rough. We're making progress, though. We're both trying to adjust to our new life and figure out how that works. It'll take time, I guess, to heal all the wounds, but I think we can make it. I know that's what my mom would want."

"I think you're right."

"It's been almost three months since . . ."

"I know. Are you doing okay?"

"I miss both of them and it still hurts, but I believe I'll see them again someday and that's what's getting me through each day. Thank you for that."

"You're welcome. Have you thought any more about the Church or the Book of Mormon?"

"I've read some more, but I need to work on things with my dad before I can make any other big decisions."

"That's probably a good idea. Take your time so you know it's the right thing to do." He smiled.

"I do plan to read all of the Book of Mormon, and I hope you'll teach me more about the Church."

"What about your dad? Do you think he's interested in learning more?"

She shrugged. "Maybe after he's dealt with everything that's happened he might be willing. I don't know. He's still struggling."

"I'll be around for a while before I leave on my mission. I have one more interview, and then I can send my papers. I should receive my call a few weeks after that."

"That's great." Liza would miss Kyle while he served his mission. She'd always be grateful to him, and his dad, for helping her to make some sense of her new life.

"My dad and I can come over anytime to talk to you and your dad." He touched her arm and the same, familiar electricity coursed through her.

"I'll let you know."

"Besides, I'll need to come over to give you my address so you can write me every week, right?" Kyle elbowed her.

Liza's dad walked over to them.

"Hello, Mr. Compton." Kyle extended his hand.

Liza's dad shook Kyle's hand.

"I better find my family. My mom wants to take more pictures. I don't know how anyone can take so many pictures." Kyle smiled. He waved as he turned and walked back toward the bleachers.

"He's a nice kid," Liza's dad said.

"Yep." She grinned.

It was funny. At the beginning of the school year, she'd ogled Kyle at the swim meets and fantasized about dating him. But now, though the attraction was still undeniable, he was no longer simply an object of her admiration—he was a close and trusted friend who'd helped her deal with an unthinkable tragedy. He'd helped her see her life in a different way and given her hope that she'd see her mom and Jason again.

Kyle was woven into the tapestry of her life and perhaps, after his mission, he'd become a permanent thread. She anticipated exploring that possibility a few years down the road.

Her dad interrupted her thoughts. "Congratulations, Liza. I'm proud of you. For everything. Can I give you a hug?"

She nodded, and she and her father embraced for the first time in a long time. She pursed her lips and struggled to keep her tears at bay. It felt even better than she remembered to have her dad's arms around her again.

Her dad said, "Are you ready to go home?"

"Yeah."

Liza and her dad walked back to their car.

As they drove away from Aldrich Heights High School, Liza reflected on her life. It was different, but it was a life worth living because she finally recognized it was filled with people she loved and that loved her.

She still had some healing to do, physically and emotionally, but she was no longer an outsider searching for her place. Though she and her dad still had a long road ahead, she felt sincerely hopeful that they could be a real family again, and, someday, they could be with her mom and Jason. Again.

About the Author

Rebecca was born and raised in Santa Barbara, California. She spent countless hours swimming in the ocean, collecting shells, and building sand castles.

She graduated from BYU with a bachelor of arts degree in communications. While attending BYU, she met and married her sweetheart, Del.

Rebecca now lives in Colorado on a small ranch with horses, goats, a dog, a cat, and a llama named Tina. She and Del have been blessed with ten creative and multi-talented children.

She has had children's stories published in online and print magazines, including the *Friend,* and is the author of the children's picture book *Grasshopper Pie.*

Besides writing, Rebecca also enjoys knitting, home redecorating, and dancing to disco music while she cleans the house. And she's consumed at least 3,541 pounds of chocolate and even more ice cream.